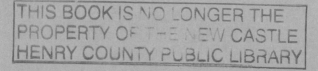

CROSSING
the TRESTLE

CROSSING
the TRESTLE

by Joseph Slate

MARSHALL CAVENDISH
New York

Grateful acknowledgment for use of the lyric excerpt
from the musical composition, SERENADE IN BLUE
by Mark Goodson and Harry Warren © 1942 (Renewed)
WB Music Corp. All Rights Reserved.
Used by Permission. WARNER BROS. PUBLICATIONS U.S. INC.,
Miami, FL. 33014.

C-1

Marshall Cavendish, 99 White Plains Road, Tarrytown, NY 10591

The text of this book is set in Berkley Old Style Medium 12/16
Printed in the United States Of America
First edition

Library of Congress Cataloging-in-Publication Data
Slate, Joseph.
Crossing the trestle / by Joseph Slate.
p. cm.
Summary: In 1944 in West Virginia, eleven-year-old Petey and his teenage one-eyed
sister wonder if their widowed mother is going to marry her friend Stone, who is a
veteran and an artist.
ISBN 0-7614-5053-x
1. World War, 1939–1945—United States—Juvenile fiction. [1. World War,
1939–1945—United States—Fiction. 2. Single-parent-family—Fiction 3. Physically
handicapped—Fiction. 4. Remarriage—Fiction. 5. Artists—Fiction.
6. West Virginia—Fiction.] I. Title.
PZ7.S6289Cr   1999   [Fic]—dc 21   98-49212   CIP   AC

1 3 5 7 8 6 4 2

FOR MY SISTERS, MARY AND LUCILLE,
AND IN MEMORIAM, DOROTHY AND ROSE.

—*the lyfe so short, the craft so long to lerne.*

Acknowledgements

For historical and technical information on eye prosthetic, I am
indebted to Dr. Geva E. Mannor, Director of Eye Plastic & Orbit
Surgery, Deparmtent of Ophthalmology, Georgetown University
Medical Center, Washington, D.C.; and Raymond Peters, master
ocularist who practices in Prince Georges County, Maryland.

The fictional Commander Soliti and Dr. Mundell generally follow procedures in use in 1944, but some of their methods may
anticipate later discoveries. Their idiosyncrasies, medical or personal, derive from the author's imagination and should not be attrib-
uted to any of my learned sources.

Also, my thanks to the following: Mollie San Tucci of the
Veterans Administration Hospital in Aspinwall, Pennsylvania; the
librarians at the Aspen Hill Library branch in Silver Spring,
Maryland, and the National Library of Medicine in Bethesda,
Maryland; and the staff of the Carnegie-Mellon Art and Natural
History Museums.

Last, but never least, my wife, Patty, who led me safely across
the trestle.

"I think you are a very bad man," said Dorothy.

"Oh no, my dear; I'm really a very good man; but I'm a very bad Wizard, I must admit."

—L. Frank Baum *The Wonderful Wizard of Oz*

CHAPTER ONE

One night, I saw Loni fall headlong off the railroad trestle into Logan Creek. I woke with a holler. Lay still, hoping I didn't wake Loni or Mom.

A faint light fanned across my window blind, then doused. The Ghost Car, its soft *pah-pah-pah* coming up from the drive down below. No lights. Always just that one faint glow and then darkness.

Mom and Loni said they never heard it. Their bedrooms were across the hall from mine, at the back of the house.

Under their bedrooms, our springer spaniel, Toby, slept. He was trained not to bark at train or car noises. He only stirred and barked if something touched the house.

"Mom says it's probably couples looking for a place to park and hold hands," I said to Loni.

"Hold hands, my nose," Loni huffed. "Probably smooching up a storm."

My *nose*. Even in West Virginia, we say my *eye*, but Loni wasn't about to call attention to her missing eye.

She sat at her drawing board, a door over two sawhorses, lettering in one of the pages of her new comic book. Loni usually drew with her left hand over her bad eye, holding her hair back. But today she was fighting the back side of a curled piece of wallpaper. Leftover wallpaper was what she drew on. She needed that hand to tame it. Her black, poker-straight hair rained down over her face. How she could see with one eye and holding her head down as she usually did was anybody's guess.

I said, "But it was pitch dark out there last night. How can anyone see without headlights? The Ghost Car never parks. I'd hear it if it stopped and started up again. Anyhow, how can a body drive and smooch, too?"

"Petey, you got to stop imagining things. Cars get lost in these old hills all the time."

Outside Loni's window, a flock of cedar waxwings was hustling our apple tree.

"Git, you bandits." I tapped on Loni's screen.

"Let them stay, Petey. They're pretty."

"They'll eat up the sets."

"If it's between waxwings and those wormy green apples we get in September, I'll take the waxwings."

September. It was almost June. School was just out, but it might as well be September with what I had to do.

"Come on, Loni," I urged. "We got to practice on the trestle. I had a nightmare about it last night, and it's all your fault."

"Again?" She sighed. "Oh, Petey."

It was an old story. My usual nightmare of being sucked down into Logan Creek. The trestle was an old wooden single-track railroad bridge held up by creosoted pilings nigh on to forty feet high. It had no railings, nothing to keep me from tripping and falling over the side. We had to cross it to get to Logan School.

I had a terrible fear of heights. Took after Mom that way. She was even stepladder shy. All I had to do was look down between the railroad ties and freeze. I was eleven—yeah, too old to need help crossing that trestle. To have Loni help me over was so embarrassing we had to pretend I was helping *her*. Loni was fourteen and had no fear of heights. Like Dad.

"Yeah, it was the trestle," I said, but I didn't say it was Loni that went over the side. Because I wasn't ever going to remind her that once she'd stopped in the middle of the trestle and said, "If I jumped, it'd be over, Petey."

"Jumped? Are you crazy? And—and what would be over?"

"Logan School. This eye."

I took a good hold of her hand.

"Aw," she said, "I'm just kidding. That ucky creek isn't worth a mortal sin. Probably be a venial sin unless I got killed."

She never said it again, but I worried. Thought I should tell Mom, but she had enough fears with Loni to have that piled on, too. And maybe Loni was just talking. She had a good sense of gallows humor.

"Just a darn minute," she said. Loni liked to imitate

Jack Benny, her favorite radio comic, and he always said that.

On her bed table, the old white Motorola—oh, it was once white, but more nearly yellow now—was sashaying into Glenn Miller's "Serenade in Blue."

I chimed in with Ray Eberle: "...sharing all the joys we used to know, many moons ago—"

"Hold it, buster," Loni yelled, her pencil up in the air, ready to strike.

It popped on the paper as she made a final dot.

Trapped in the jungles of Gula, Darryl and Hedy fight off a giant four-eyed Helix. One bite means death!

"Sounds like Flesh Gordon," I said. Alex Raymond was Loni's favorite artist, next to John Neill of the scary Oz books.

"*Flash. Flash* Gordon," Loni corrected. "Flesh means skin. You wouldn't call someone Skin Gordon, would you?"

"We call him Flesh in school."

"Half the kids in Logan School are ignoramuses," Loni said. "Glad I'm never going back. And I'll have you know I do not copy Flash Gordon. Not directly. And don't you ever tell Stone that I do."

"I won't because I never said that you did."

Stone Gardner was a hurt veteran lately come from Seattle to do a picture mural for Cokin Steel. He rented a side house from our landlord, Gen Geeter, up on Gen's farm on the hill west of us. He took a shine to Loni because they were both artists, I guess, although he liked me, too, and I couldn't draw a straight line with a ruler.

"And Petey, don't you think it's time you watched the way you talk, your grammar and all? You sound like a hoopie."

She drew a real neat balloon around the words she lettered, and then snapped her yellow drawing pencil into a tray packed tight with pens and such. Then she slid the tray into the top hollow of the marbled box they gave her in Wheeling Hospital. There were four trays, the blue paper peeling off all of them, filled with compasses, protractors, triangles, and other torments they stick in pencil boxes for kids never to use.

Loni squared off her pencil box to one side of her drawing board. Then she began to slap a row of her art stuff into line.

That clutter was under her art-prize ribbons tacked to the wall over her drawing door. *Wham!* went a catalog of wallpaper samples. *Wham!*—a cigar box of yarn. *Wham!* a pint Mason jar of brushes and scissors. *Wham, wham, wham!* two black tins of watercolors, a box of Crayolas, and a tub of paste. When they were all lined up like soldiers, I gave a salty General MacArthur salute.

"You said it, buster." She nodded, laughing.

It was good to make Loni laugh.

"I haint goin' change the way I talk," I said, using a downstate West Virginia twang and throwing in haint, which Loni hated. "Not upstate hoity-toity."

"Better be careful, Petey. Dint Mom tell you your mouth could get stuck that way? Near fatal for someone who wants to be a famous Walt Disney writer."

She waved her hand back to the shelves against the wall. There, her Oz and Mark Twain books, most with their perfect covers, sat backing her up, daring me to do better.

"I don't write the way I talk. And I'll have you know I get my best grades in composition. If I talked like you wanted me to talk, I'd be beaten up in school every day. Anyway, someone who says dint for didn't every time she turns around shouldn't throw stones."

"Listen, Petey, I don't *mean* to say dint. It slips out. I know it's wrong. Miss Gumm says what counts is *knowing* when you're wrong and trying to fix it. In the fall, Miss Gumm will get after you fast if you give her any of that hoopie stuff. She's one big elbow."

"I'd just as soon forget about Miss Gumm and school."

She pushed back the secretary chair Mom got from the Salvation Army. Its crabbed wheels sounded like it was crushing the flowers in the linoleum.

"Well, you can't forget about the trestle," she said, snapping off Glenn Miller. "Petey, you got to learn."

"Well, I know I do. But I wouldn't have to this soon if you were going back to Logan in the fall. You only have one more year before they ship you off to Cokinville High. Can't see why you couldn't just stick with Logan through your last grade here."

It was a peculiar set-up, having a school with only ten grades and then sending us off to a new school for the final two grades. But it saved the county from building a new high school for us hillies, since Logan had enough room for ten grades.

"How many times, Petey, have you had to say to someone to stop staring at me? How many times?"

"They only stare when you take off that patch. 'Cause your eye—you know—kind of runs sometimes. When you get a cold? And they only call you names when you fight. Loni, you are real pretty—honest. If you'd get a glass eye—"

"Oh, sure, and thank you, mister. And how pretty do you think I'd look, goggle-eyed with a fake eye popping out of my head? They'd stare just as much. So please, Petey, let me just stay home in peace. I kept up fine with my studies once I got out of Wheeling Hospital. And I have a right."

She had a right all right. Even the County Extension lady said they had to allow it until Loni felt right or got a glass eye. And Mom was retreating.

"Six white horses comin' 'round the mountain couldn't drag her back," Mom said, sighing. "Let's face it, Loni *wants* to stay home. I don't know how long they'll let County Extension send off lessons, but for now, she's dug in her heels. And oh I dread to think— well, I won't think it and I won't say it."

The hallway sang out as we pounded down the steps, Loni's drawing satchel bumping the stair rail. But she was careful of the wall. I could still smell the paste from the new wallpaper she and Mom put up the week before. It mixed in powerfully with the heavy, sweet smell of the locust blossoms that slapped on the window screen landing.

Toby was waiting at the bottom, twisting his behind right up to his stubbed-off tail. His speckled black and white feathering did a hula with his shaking. *Take me, take me.*

"And where, may I ask, is your eye patch?" Mom said.

Loni swept her hand over her head, so that a fall of black, shiny hair covered her bad eye.

"Oh, Mom, if people don't like it, they can lump it. It's too hot for that ugly old eye patch. I don't care what anybody thinks."

"Honey, you have a drawer full of pretty eye patches. If you're going to be tramping around in the woods, you don't want to get a briar or whiplash in that eye. Is it in the drawing satchel?"

"No, it's in my pocket!" Loni said, slapping the front of Dad's old white dress shirt. That was what she wore almost every single summer day. That and an old pair of floppy, tan Sears, Roebuck slacks.

"Anyhow, I wouldn't be tramping through the woods if Petey would learn to walk the trestle on his own."

Mom sighed, stretched her arms, lifted and flicked the long black pony tail off her neck. Now that her arms were up she began to swivel on the piano stool she bought at auction. Was she about to sing?

Toby thought so. He slid under the sewing machine and chomped down on her slipper.

If you're goin' ta sing, you got to get up and dance, was what he meant. We often wondered if he was a circus dog, dropped off along the railroad tracks where Dad found him. If you dared hum or looked about to dance, Toby would worry your shoes until you shut up or really danced.

You gotta mooooove, he seemed to say.

"Stop that, Toby," Mom said, kicking.

"Seems to me, honey," she said, trying to jiggle back into her pulled slipper, "if you set your mind to going back to school, Petey wouldn't have to walk that trestle himself so soon. They're not going to bring back short-haul school buses until after gas rationing, although I did read that Eleanor Roosevelt is making a fuss about it. And we can't afford to move, even if there was a place to move to. This war! So what's the answer?"

"It's not me," Loni replied. "I'm not going back, and they can't make me. I am physically deee-formed."

"Honey," Mom said gently," I wish you wouldn't say that. You do not come under any such rubric. But as long as you fight, I guess they won't. Look, it's time we saw a specialist about your eye. Dr. Berdelli—that sainted man, God keep his soul, delivered you both without a hitch"—Mom paused, ducked down to adjust her slipper—"told me they were doing all kinds of wonders now with eye surgery for the wounded boys, and now I read there's a new *plastic* eye, they say, that's—"

"Mom, I don't care. And please, I don't want to talk about plastic eyes. I feel like a freak as it is." She spun 'round with her drawing satchel and slammed out the door.

"Hold Toby, Mom," I said. I gave her one sorrowful look before following after Loni.

CHAPTER TWO

Out-of-staters like to call West Virginians ridge runners. We don't much dignify that, but since most of our towns are in river valleys and hollows, we got no choice but to run our houses up the sides of hills, especially since much of the valley flatland is business—highways, steel mills, stores, and such.

Our house above Geeter Hollow was no different. It's about three-quarters down Geeter Hill. Oh, outsiders call Geeter Hill a mountain, but we're given to cutting our mountains down to size, since we live right *in* them.

Here's the way I told it to a kid who was supposed to be my pen pal, but never became a pal because he never answered.

If you laid a clock face over the whole of Logan Valley, Geeter Hill would be at high noon, our house'd be at nine, the trestle would be at six, and the Ohio River and its bridges would be at three.

Logan Creek and the Pennsy east-west railroad tracks would run straight across that clock from three to nine. So does the path we followed high above the tracks. Like most all the paths on Geeter Hill, it leads to the foot overpass and the trestle. The overpass is about the center of the clock.

I liked the overpass. It was used by us hillies and Pennsy Railroad workers to cross from one side of about a thousand tracks to the trestle, which was a shortcut to Logan and school. If you dropped a plumb line straight down from the trestle and off my clock map at six o'clock, Logan school is what you'd hit.

Loni strummed her walking stick along the meshy guardrail fence of the overpass. Being so closed in, the height never bothered me. Nor did the tiny plank holes underfoot.

"Do you think we'll see some lucky white boxcars go under us today?" I asked Loni.

"I hope so," Loni said. "I got plenty of wishes."

Day after day, the trains whistled through our skinny slice of West Virginia panhandle at high wartime speed. On to Ohio west, on to Pennsylvania east. But at that moment, there were no long trains in sight. Just fix-up crews. A locomotive on the far side was switching tracks.

The engineer saw us and waved his gloved hand, fringed and starred, cowboy to cowboys. Oh, we knew what he would do! Chug, chug, chug—he shot up a dense cloud of smoke, making us invisible. Loni whooped and hollered, startling me.

"We're invisible, Petey!" she cried, whirling around in the smoke like the witch in the movie, *The Wizard of Oz*. She loved being out of sight. Loved magicians with their vanishing acts. Dark movie houses and such.

After the overpass, we followed a clear lay of gravel and narrow, rusty track marks. The tracks leading up to the trestle had been torn up for the war effort.

"Dang, Petey," Loni said, "they could have told us those tracks were for scrap. We would have cleaned up."

"Cripe's sakes, Loni, we couldn't lift a whole track."

"Don't be so sure. Dint—*didn't*—we get that piece down from Gen Geeter's?"

"A yea lot of good it did us. I just about got ruptured."

Once off the overpass, we stood before Logan Creek trestle. The scarey trestle. Dingeys, little locomotives with dinging bells, used to cross it from a slag mill on the other side of the creek, but now with the lead-in tracks tore up, it was for hillies like us.

As Loni was about to step out on the trestle, the ground shook and thunder rolled up behind us.

We spun 'round to wave as a troop train shot by. Khaki-sleeved arms waved back through open windows. In a minute the soldiers were gone, leaving only the sad hum of the rails, shiny as tears. I thought of Dad's razor, stropped fine.

And then I thought of Dad. Standing in front of the kitchen sink, in his Clark Gable undershirt. His tanned arm rippled as his hand stroked the razor against the strap. He did it right fine, a lapping water motion. His fingers held the razor like a thin wafer.

"You'll have to do this someday, Petey," he said, laughing.

I loved him, but never could say it much. I mean, he knew I thought he was the world and all, but to have to say that was embarrassing. So he never said it either. We knew.

Loni broke into my woolgathering. "Petey, now you got to pay attention."

"Do you ever wonder why'd it have to happen, Loni?"

"What happen?" Loni was anxious to get me trained on the trestle so she could set out to draw it. She wanted to surprise Stone with a good sketch. I could tell she was thinking of him, maybe up on Geeter's rock where he sometimes drew. She began digging into her shirt pocket for her wadded black eye patch.

"Help me with this," she said. She pressed out the little sack that fit over her eye and drew on the elastic band that held it in place. Then she slipped it over her head. She swung the patch around to cover her eye. Her hair stood up on the back of her head like a Chinese fan.

"Tuck my hair under, Petey," she said. She stooped so I could reach.

I slipped her hair under the band and tucked in some strays. She gripped a fall of side hair. Fixed it under the band so that it covered part of the eye patch. It didn't hide it. Only made her look like Geronimo.

But my mind was still on the accident. "It happened right over yonder, didn't it? Loni, *didn't* it?"

"Oh, for gosh sakes, Petey!" Her good hazel eye stared a hole in me. "Okay."

She slapped down her drawing satchel and sat hard

on the gravel bank overlooking Logan Creek, not caring a whit about dirtying her slacks. Then she slowly turned her head all the way west. She pointed over to the Pennsy railroad bridge and its twin, the Fort Holliday, which was only for cars.

I knew that's where the accident happened, but I needed to hear it again.

"It was right there. See yonder where the bridge goes right into the bank, on the Ohio side? You have to make a sharp right, and that's where we hit the ice patch. The car went 'round and 'round. Dad put his arm out to hold me back on the seat, but that's all I can recall.

"He dint say a thing," Loni added, sniffing.

I could tell I was setting Loni off when she didn't correct herself saying dint.

"I guess we better let it drop," I said, but it was like picking at a scab. I couldn't.

I said, "Dad'd clench his teeth and pitch right in to save it if he could."

"Except he couldn't," Loni said. "Not on ice. We spun into the bridge stone and bounced head on to the other side. He dint feel anything, Petey..."

Loni's head went down and her shoulders began to shake.

"Well, he dint, he dint!" Loni choked out, giving my arm a good slap with the back of her hand. "He dint feel one thing, the doctors said."

Dang her! Her slap knocked the tears right out of my

eyes and down my cheeks. We just sat there like two hounds a-bawling like blue bejeebers. We had nothing but our sleeves to wipe away the run of our faces.

I could never understand how Dad or anybody could get killed and not feel anything.

"You know, Loni, I think if I was there, maybe it would of happened another way. I mean, if you didn't have to go to get your tonsils painted and I weren't sick in bed, Mom and me would of been there, you'd of been in back, and—"

Loni broke in, "And then Mom would have been beat up like me, so stop thinking about it. It ain't—isn't—good, thinking about it. And especially around Mom you should shut up about it."

"I guess."

"You should. Start thinking about how you're going to get yourself over this trestle for school is what you should start thinking about. And Petey, tie those gym shoes."

It wasn't just that brute trestle. Logan Creek was a boiling stream of foaming pickling acid, drowned cats, and garbage. I looked west over my gym shoes; that stuff left a trial of white shore scum all the way down to the Ohio River.

I guess I looked pretty dismal, because Loni changed her tune.

"Now, Petey," she said, honey dripping from her tongue, "you couldn't fall if you tried. Try closing one eye."

"You go ahead. I got to gear up."

"You can't just fly up and pop over the side, for gosh sakes," Loni said. "You can't fall through the ties. You can't fit between those ties without catching your arms."

"You go ahead!" I shouted. "Go on."

Loni had no fear, not of heights, anyway. She skipped right to the middle of the trestle before I could blink. Her slacks flapped in the breeze as she cased the steaming water below. If she ever had a mind to jump, she had the grit to do it, that was for sure.

Then suddenly, she was gone. I knew where she must be, but her disappearance never failed to scare me.

"Loni, I know where you are!"

A hand, chipped red painted nails, waved up from between the ties.

She was in the well, a cradle under the ties for workmen to hie to in case a dingey came over.

Laughing, she pried herself up and skipped toward me.

"Dang those rails are hot," she said, dancing back to me.

"Now don't look down. I'll lead you."

"I don't want you to lead me." I was ticked at her showing off by jumping in the well.

"I don't want you looking at me while I try walking this. I'm going to try Stone's bamboo pole notion and see if that works."

"Okay, okay." Loni backed off. She started monkeying with her eye patch at the mention of Stone's name.

"I'm not going to look at you. I'm going to sit on this end and draw with my head down." She shook her drawing pad at me. "Is that okay?"

"You'll peek," I said.

"For Pete's sake!" Loni yelled, getting up and glaring at me.

"I'll draw the trestle from below if that makes you feel any better. And I hope you trip on those dumb shoelaces. Now please, Petey, tie them right now."

She sloshed into the ankle-deep slag that sloped down to a ledge halfway above the creek.

"Listen, Loni," I yelled, "I wouldn't have to do this if you'd go back to school."

"You listen," Loni yelled back. "I can't be holding your hand my whole life. Gee whiz, Petey, you have three whole months."

I guess I shouldn't be so tetchy. Loni slipping and sloshing down to the ledge would upset Mom. It wasn't that she'd fall in, but the fumes were enough to kill a skunk. I wasn't about to call her back.

I retied my gym shoes and set out. I held the bamboo pole like Stone told me, just as I'd seen high-wire circus people do. Heads up and toes pointed out. I paused before each step.

Of course, I was peeking down, so as not to trip. It went fine until I got over the deep fall-off part. Then's when I began to get tingling hands and short breath.

"Listen," I said to myself, panting. "Look down only

when you step, and then look up fast."

That gave me about five steps more, about to the safety well at the halfway point. If I could make that, I could rest without getting dizzy. The well under the tracks blanked out the creek. It was deep and wide enough to crowd two workmen if a dingey was coming. But before that point, my eyes drifted over the edge.

"Ahhhhhh." I froze. My heart hop-danced. I began to pant.

Stone told me to take big gulps of air and blow them out, in and out, to relax. That helped a little, but as I raised my head to start again, I gasped.

Marching toward me was the pudgy Dead End bully we only knew as Olenk. Once before, he tried running me off the bridge, but Loni gaped her eye at him, struck him, and just spooked the heck out of him. Now he was with one of his pals, a tall, gangly kid with a skeleton face I'd not seen before. He wasn't likely to be spooked again.

My heart began to pound so, I thought it'd jump right out of my mouth. One fear raced the other. I knew I didn't have the nerve to turn and jump the ties back. I had to get to the safety well or I'd be a goner.

"Oh, God, oh, Dad, move my legs!" I prayed. Shameful as it was, I crouched down and duck-walked the three more ties to the well.

I jumped between the ties, into the well. Splinters burned my arm.

I tried to find a hole to push the bamboo pole through, but could only wedge it into the open seam of the iron cradle. Then I gripped my knees around it. A good half of it stuck up above the ties.

Right soon, I heard Olenk's mean play-acting voice.

"Hey, I wonder who left this bamboo pole sticking up like that," he said, spitting down on me.

"A body might trip, don't you think, Skeetz? I better pull that right up out of the way. Ah, gee, look who's down in the well—ol' sis. And the ol' one-eye witch isn't here to help him cross the widdle bridge."

I felt the pole wiggle.

"Hey, Skeetz," Olenk said, "I always wanted a bamboo pole."

"Let go," I shouted. "I ain't letting go."

I meant it. I had a good anchor and I wasn't about to give up on my bamboo pole.

"Ah, the widdle sis ain't letting go," Olenk chided in a baby voice as he rocked the pole.

Through a slit in the metal cradle, I could see Loni look up. She was on the far side of the creek. Olenk and Skeetz had come from the other side. Being almost under the trestle, could she see or hear them?

"Give it up, give it up," Olenk shouted, "or I'll break it off."

"Let's piss on him," Skeetz said. "Then he'll let go."

"What is it?" Loni yelled. "Who's up there, Petey?"

"It's that rat Olenk," I shouted. "He's after my pole."

"Rat, rat," Olenk shouted, tugging and twisting, "who's a rat?"

I could see Loni staggering up the slag pile, the loose gravel sucking at her ankles.

"Leave him be!" Loni shouted.

Olenk and Skeetz both put their weight on the bamboo pole. I clamped my legs as tight as I could. The pole's pressure hurt sorely as it lifted my thigh. I was never going to give in, even if it broke my leg.

Suddenly, the old bamboo snapped and splintered. A split stung through my palms like lightning. It hummed through my knees and twisted the skin on my thigh.

Olenk's shadow fell back. I heard a thud. Did he fall? I wished he had, right over the trestle.

"You rats, you broke it," I shouted. Tears smarted my eyes. My mouth was dry. I rose up in a red fury with what was now only a spear.

Loni came agalloping over the ties, shouting at Olenk, who was being pulled up by Skeetz. Her patch was slightly twisted half off her eye.

"Uh-oh," Olenk shouted, spinning around, "here comes the Queen of Halloween!"

He jumped a tie and pointed the other half of the bamboo spear at Loni.

"You come closer," he growled, "I'll put out your other eye." Last time, when Loni gaped her hollow eye at Olenk, she also struck him with a tree limb, sending him reeling and acting sick. But she daren't now. She had no weapon to fend him off.

I couldn't help. Skeetz and Olenk were between me and Loni. I was stuck half in and half out of the well. I'd have to drop the spear, lean forward, and hoist myself up.

Then I saw a figure way off on the overpass. It was Stone, his hat in his hand. He was running toward us, black spyglasses swinging from a cord 'round his neck. I shouted, "Loni, here comes Dad!"

That routed them. Olenk threw the bamboo over the side. He and Skeetz whirled and run, knocking me to the side. I felt Skeetz's clodhoppers hard on my hand.

CHAPTER THREE

"That was good thinking, Petey," Loni said, helping me walk back by taking hold of one side of my bamboo spear, "calling Stone Dad."

I didn't say it, but I felt a hollow in me. Stone was good enough to be a Dad. But not good enough to be our Dad. "Sorry, Dad," I prayed under my breath.

Stone walked toward us, his black hair all spiked out, a worried look on his bearded, lopsided face.

"Hell's bells," he called, breathing hard, "are you kids all right?"

"Stone," I shouted, holding up the spear, "guess what! You were right. Using that bamboo pole helped get me to the well."

"I s-saw that," he said. Sometimes Stone stuttered, but not enough for anyone to notice. "Watched. But what was all that commotion about?" Stone swallowed hard; his Adam's apple rode up and down on his whiskery neck.

"Those rats wanted my bamboo pole. I wouldn't let go. So they broke it off, but it took two of them."

"You all right, Pete?" Stone repeated.

"Yeah," I said, showing my bruised arm and red hands. "I got spit on. A few splinters. They said they'd put Loni's eye out."

"Holy moly, who the hell are those hoodlums?"

"Don't know," Loni said. "One, that Olenk one's been here before by himself. He wasn't so nervy then. I ran him off. I guess he likes to search the tracks for junk. Thinks he owns it all."

"Stone," I asked, "how did you know we were here?"

"I called your Mom. Said you little beavers went right back to work. Looked to me from Geeter's Rock you were doing okay."

"Did you watch us through the spyglasses?" I asked.

"*Binoculars*, Petey," Loni corrected.

"I know it," I said, "but spyglasses is a more exciting word if you think about it."

Stone grinned and nodded.

"Petey said you were our Dad," Loni replied.

"You did, Pete? You devil." He cocked his head and held his thumbs up like horns. His left hand trembled a bit, but the right one held steady. Stone had the darnest fingers—long, but crooked every one.

"I hope Dad—*you*—didn't mind that," I said. Dang, I almost said what I felt.

"Mind. Hell—ssssh-shoot, no! There's more than one way to skin a cat."

"Too bad I dint—*didn't*—too have time to skin them," Loni said. "I'd have told them you were up there watching with binoculars every time Petey walks the trestle."

"Yeah," I said, "with a sighted rifle."

"A battleship howitzer," Loni said.

"A Big Bertha!" I added.

Oh, we could've gone on with a lying good list if Stone hadn't got serious.

"Your Mom said you were drawing the trestle down here," Stone said to Loni. "That's a wise idea, Loni. To see a thing from every angle. Your wallpaper comic books are pretty wonderful, but it's good to get back to things and nature."

"Her new one's just like Flesh Gordon," I said.

"Petey," Loni said sternly, "you know that's Flash, not *Flesh*. He just *says* that!"

Stone did his one-grunt laugh. "I'd say he's Flash and flesh. Sh-shoot. He keeps losing his clothes, he's going to be all flesh."

"Hey, that's a hot one," I said, and I had to laugh out loud. Stone was a crackerjack guy. Even Loni had to smile at that.

"Oh, heavens," Loni said. She turned 'round and headed down the slag. "I left my pad and pencils on that rock."

"Dint—*didn't*—get much done," Loni said, after fetching her drawing. She handed it to Stone.

"Ah, that's very hard." Stone studied it. "To get perspective right from underneath a structure as complex as a trestle. I have a little book on perspective drawing that might help, but it's not the end all or be all of drawing. I like this as is. You really got the feel of the brute nature of this thing."

"I'm going to do some more drawing on the rock

this afternoon," Loni hinted. "And tomorrow."

"Me, too," I said to Stone. "I think I'll try, too."

"Why not?" Stone didn't say he'd be there either today or tomorrow, and Loni looked disappointed. Stone was working hard on his mural for Cokin Steel.

We headed for the foot overpass. I ran. Stone and Loni followed after. Halfway across I stopped to see if any trains were coming, waiting for Loni and Stone to catch up.

A tiny yellow butterfly zigzagged over my hand and lighted on the rail. But the metal was burning hot. Poor critter, shot off sideways like a school note flipped off a thumb.

As we neared the path side of the bridge, there was a loud, shattering slam. Some engine coupling, but half under us.

Loni and me stopped to look down. I turned to see if Stone had joined us to watch the coupling. But he wasn't with us. He was across from us, against the guardrail fence, crouched down. His shoulder was pressed into the mesh. His hands were over his head. His shoulders were shaking something fierce.

I turned and stared at Loni. She stared wildly back at me, a hand over her mouth. Then suddenly Stone looked up. He gaped his sunken brown eyes like he'd just woke up. His tanned face was purply gray against his spittled black beard. His mouth was open, sucking air.

"Stone. Mighten you be sick?" Loni asked.

He shook his head, his mouth still open, and then

pulled himself slowly up by the top rail.

"It was n-nothing, nothing. I—only a cramp. I better hustle back."

He jumped out ahead of us. I noticed he was wearing his moccasins. Right soon, he was moving up the path as fast as any movie Indian, although he wasn't one, just an ex-G.I. from Seattle.

We didn't go up to the rock at all. We were worried about Stone and needed to tell Mom what happened.

"I hope Gen Geeter's home," Loni said. "Maybe he needs a doctor."

"Gen Geeter's always spying," I said. "He'd see Stone go into that studio, don't you think?"

"But he wouldn't know he was sick," Loni said. "Maybe Mom should call Gen."

"Oh, I don't think Mom'll do that, Loni."

CHAPTER FOUR

At home, Toby greeted us at the door with one yelp.
Then he whirled back to Mom, who was sewing in the
good dining room. He was a regular Simon Legree,
making sure Mom kept treadling. And poor Mom, she
dared not sing.

If you're going to sew, sew! is the way he looked at it.
And if you're going to sing, dance!

Legs frogged out, he reminded me of a black and
white Walt Disney cartoon mop, jerking his head with
Mom's every treadle.

"Mom, we're back," Loni yelled, swiping Toby.

Did she hear? The sewing machine whined, and she
kept her head down. Her eyes were on the needle.

Her brow was creased to give herself nerve as she
spun a skirt hem around a flickering dart. Even before
the car wreck, she had a caution about machines.

Still and all, it was the Singer sewing machine, Dad's
insurance money, and Cokin Steel pension that kept her
at home. Mom's sewing, mostly alterations for Brown's
cleaners and sometimes drapes and chair covers for
Tulli's, was stacked all around her. What she liked was
dressmaking. She made all her own clothes without even
so much as a pattern. And Loni's, too. But there wasn't
much call for that up in Cokinville or down here in
Geeter's Hollow.

"Mom-om!" Loni was right up to Mom's ear.

"Geeszoy!" Mom said, jumping. Her eyes, cobalt blue, were shining moist, so I knew she had been crying. Aside the piano stool lay one of Dad's shirts, a threaded needle stuck through it. She kept them mended for Loni, though she never got through a rip without crying.

"You startled me. Look, honey, Denny's going to be here in an hour, and I've got four skirts to take in. What is it?"

Denny Dorfapple, Brown's driver—he was 4-F because of a fricasseed kidney or something—helped Mom load the van twice a week. Then she'd ride back with him. He was shy to speechless. If I was writing up Denny for Walt Disney, I'd make him a stork. He was always delivering things for Mom. He'd do about anything for her. Pick up sewing, help her carry groceries, and wait for her while she picked up books at the Cokinville library.

Mom had only gone to seventh grade—pulled out of school when her Dad died, to help *her* mom tend boarders—but with Dad's help, she educated herself just fine. She was always on the library list for the latest biographies and novels. Read the whole of *Gone with the Wind*, if you can imagine that.

"It's Stone, Mom," Loni said.

Mom snapped a thread with her teeth and looked over her shoulder at Loni.

"I know, honey," Mom said. "Oh, I don't know. Oh,

I couldn't think. He's been so ding-darn nice to you kids. He wanted to take me out to dinner."

Loni bit her lower lip, looking like she was ready to bust out crying.

"Mom-om," Loni whined. She took off her eye patch and began rubbing the sweat crease across her forehead.

"You dint—didn't—say no again, did you?"

"Well geeszoy, what could I say? Well, I hope you don't mind. Honey, I don't know what in heaven we'd talk about with my puny scarecrow education. And he's not that easy around me, either."

"It's only his being shy, Mom," Loni said. "He's real easy around me and Petey."

I liked Stone a yea lot, but I didn't want Mom going out with anyone.

"Yes, he is," I said, "but something's wrong. He got real sick today."

"Sick?" Mom stopped treadling. Toby dived at her toe.

"It was just a cramp," Loni said, glaring at me.

Mom said to Toby, "I'm finished for now, Toby, if your Royal Highness doesn't mind." She pushed at her back.

Toby snorted into the rug and rolled his eyes.

"Now, Loni, tell me what happened."

"Go ahead, Petey," Loni said, "you were on the trestle first."

I must say I put a fine spin on it, giving myself goose bumps as I wound up.

"...And then, Mom, then, Olenk made fun of Loni's eye patch. The dummy must a thought she was wearing a Halloween mask. Called her the Queen of Halloween. Said he'd put out her other eye."

"Now that is vim vicious," Mom said. "Slice it any which way, I have had enough of this. I am going to call the sheriff and this hoodleloom's parents, if he has parents, which I wouldn't bet a tinkle on. But then what happened?"

"Petey was the hero," Loni said. She told how I yelled out Dad, how Stone came running, and where he got sick. When Loni was through, Mom shot over to the telephone book.

"Stone's temporary number's 9-K, Mom," Loni said.

"Oh, no," Mom said, "I'm not going to call Stone. He's probably embarrassed to the nines. He'd have to been through an awful lot to be on permanent disability. He doesn't say it, but what I've read—" She stopped and looked away from the phone book.

"Or maybe it was what Stone said it was—a cramp."

She folded open the phone book. "What I'm looking for is Olenk, if there's such a thing as an Olenk listed."

"He's not someone from school, Mom," Loni said. "They're down from Cokinville, I bet."

She beamed in at the O's, but there was no Olenk.

"Maybe they don't have a phone," she said. "Someone like that's had no upbringing. Just a dingle-dangle. Now kids, I've told you before I don't want you on the trestle alone. It sounds to me like it's becoming a testing ground for hoodlelooms and other bad apples from up and down this valley. I'm going to call Sheriff Quantico. If he can't do anything, I better give Gen Geeter notice about renting elsewhere, but only God knows where. Meanwhile, I don't want either one of you alone on that trestle unless Stone is up on the rock."

"If Stone's sick," I said, "do you think he'll be able to take you out to dinner?"

"Petey, I didn't say he was taking me out to dinner."

"Oh, but Mom, you never go out," Loni said. "You look so nice when you dress up."

"Geeszoy," Mom said. "Look who's singing Dixie. I can say the same about you, honey."

Mom thumbed through to the directory, looking for Sheriff Quantico's number, I figgered.

"But getting back to Stone," she said, "what I did was say I wouldn't go *out* to dinner, but I did ask him to come *here* for dinner. I told him to invite one of his hospital friends when he's up there in Pittsburgh next. It should make conversation flow easier."

CHAPTER FIVE

Too much Kool-Aid.

In the middle of the night, I stumbled into the bathroom. Just as I started to take a leak, I heard the Ghost Car, the laboring *pah-pah-pah* through the screen. I whipped around, sending a jet against the bathtub.

Dang! Too late. As I lifted the blind, a faint light winked in the darkness, danced 'round, and huffed off at the bend.

Back in bed, I had a nice thought. Maybe it was Dad's ghost, tooling around as happy as Toby with two stub tails, keeping watch on us. That set me to sleep.

In the morning, I sat on Loni's bed, giving her my thinking. She was in a good mood because we were going up to Geeter Rock, where Stone was going to give her an art lesson.

She looked right smart, bent over her drawing board, wearing a pink blouse Mom had made. Her Sears, Roebuck tan slacks were pressed to a faretheewell. And she had a fresh eye patch—a blue satin one with Mom's stitching making an x that puckered at the center. All for Stone.

"Loni," I said. "I swear to goodness I saw the Ghost Car last night, just the light, but I looked too late from the bathroom window. And you know what I decided? I decided it's Dad, tooling around, keeping his eye on us."

Loni fixed her hazel eye on me. It had a blue rim the color of Mom's eyes. Real pretty. She smiled. I tended to forget how pretty Loni was when she smiled. She had Dad's perfect teeth, just like me.

"Oh, Petey, that is such a good thought. That's the nicest idea. You should tell Mom."

Boy! Stone was working wonders with Loni's disposition, that was for sure.

I leaned over her shoulder and read out loud the balloon she'd circled in: "'Darryl hears Hedy scream and turns to see the fiendish Vinards sweep her into the air.'"

"That's pronounced 'feen,'" she said, "not 'fine.' It's a hard word to say. *Feen*-dish."

"Fiendish," I said, showing my teeth. I knew what it meant from reading Flesh Gordon, but never had to say it out loud.

Loni asked, "Do you think I should take one of my comics up to Stone?"

"He could give you some ideas," I said. "It would fit in my satchel with the drawings."

"How about this one," Loni held up "The Adventures of Roger and Felicia." They looked like Darryl and Hedy, but Darryl had black hair this time and Hedy red.

"It looks good," I said. "The cover is one of your best."

"No," Loni said, "I'll wait until he comes for dinner and surprise him. Now don't tell."

"Cross my heart and hope to die."

Downstairs, Loni stood in front of the hallway looking glass, fiddling with the patch. Then she pulled at the
front of her blouse like it was too tight or something.
Mom said Loni was beginning to grow into a young lady
and was moody about it all.

"Mom, do you think this blouse could be let out?"
Loni called out. "It's real pretty, but..."

Mom came in from the kitchen. "Honey, that's perfect for you. Heavens, you can't go around in Dad's shirts
the rest of your life. You want to look nice don't you?"

"Yeah, like a one-eyed beauty queen," Loni said,
sarcasticlike. "Queen of Halloween, that's me."

Then she began pumping her shoulders like Bette
Davis, screwing up her face like James Cagney, and
doing a whole bunch of other jerky movie star set-ups.
Her favorites were the Dead End Kids, even though she
saw their movies with Dad two hundred years ago at the
second-run Strand.

"Hey, Petey," she said, telling me for the umpty-
umpth time about what Bobby Jordan or one of them
says about stealing a bathtub.

"There was a tootsie in the tub, but she wouldn't
come wit' me," she growled, gooshing up her mouth in
the looking glass. That always got us. We staggered into
the sewing room and fell back on the studio couch,
laughing our heads off.

"Okay, hyenas," Mom said. "Off with the both of
you."

We trooped along One-Mile Path to Gen Geeter's farm, and halfway up we veered off to Geeter's Rock. Stone was sitting on the edge, his legs dangling over, gazing out over the valley, sketching scenes for his mural. No pipe showing, but its sweet scent filled the air.

"Now act nonchalant," Loni said. That was her favorite new word. She said it meant acting like nothing special. Pretending.

We tiptoed from the woods onto the rock's mossy surface and moseyed nonchalant up behind him. Not too close—you could never get me close to the edge of that rock—trying to get a good peek at his sketchbook.

Stone turned before we were speaking distance.

It was hard to make him out. A bill cap shaded his bearded face and pilot's sunglasses. But his teeth flashed through in a smile. So we stepped right out toward him.

Stone picked off his sunglasses and slipped them into his khaki shirt pocket. He slapped down his Pittsburgh Paint cap and wiped a white handkerchief over the sweat crease across his high, bony forehead. About wiped his whole face. Puffed his cheeks and scrubbed his beard so it stood right out on its ends. He reminded me of a drawing of a whiskery otter in one of Loni's books, coming up for air. Yeah, an otter is what I'd make Stone if I were doing his part for Walt Disney. 'Course, it wouldn't work when the air went out of his cheeks. He was too thin.

"Look here," he said to Loni. "I have something for you." He reached under a drawing pad and slid a square of window glass out from between two pieces of gray cardboard. "I'm going to take you right through a whole drawing then maybe you can do a painting from it."

He handed Loni the glass. It was rimmed with black tape and had black crisscross lines drawn on it.

"Now think of that grid as your picture. Walk around the rock until you see all you'd like to fit into that glass frame. Then we'll work from there."

Loni held up the glass with both hands like she was looking out a window. She tilted it down off the edge of the rock. There were spring beauties, a slopeful of them, stars trailing to a ledge below.

Loni shifted from the flowers to the trestle below.

"Would the trestle be too hard?" she asked.

"Would you like to do it?" Stone said. "I always find it's as easy doing hard as it is doing easy. Same problem, and you feel better if you whip the hard one."

First, though, he had Loni mark off and draw the same crisscross lines on a larger piece of drawing paper, but with bigger spaces between. She had to do it without even a ruler. That took so long and was so boring, I got an itch to go down to the trestle.

Then I decided I better not try walking it by myself. I sat by Stone, but back from the edge. He was sketching, real dead serious, not a blink to his eyes, jerking his head over and back from Loni, a little like Toby when he was on to Mom's treadling.

"Stone," I said, "I did pretty good with that bamboo pole you gave me, but I was still...well, spooked."

"It wasn't a fair shoot, Petey," Stone said, fumbling for something in his pocket. He was giving Loni quick looks as he sketched. I wondered if he knew Loni didn't like anyone taking her picture.

"But even if Olenk didn't menace us," I continued, "I don't think I would of got as far as I did. Tell me, why can't people do what they want to do? Just once, I'd like to walk that dang trestle by myself. If I want to do it, why does my insides say I can't? Who's the boss, me or my insides?"

"It scares ya, huh?" Stone whispered like he didn't want to embarrass me before the world.

"I'm all right until the slag drops off, and then I'm pretty all right until I get to the big drop. Then I can't move. Like I'm going to be sucked right down. I wish there was a wizard like in Loni's *Wizard of Oz*. You know, the lion went to him for courage?"

Loni looked up from her drawing.

"Petey," she said, "the wizard really dint—didn't— give him courage. The wizard was a humbug. The lion just believed the wizard gave him courage to make him forget he was afraid.

A red-tailed hawk soared over us. Two sparrows were pestering it like flies. It dove behind a fringe of willow aside Catfish Pond. Rid of him, the sparrows wheeled back toward us.

Stone said, "I'll tell you, I get a little like that in an elevator or any tight closed-in space."

"Really? Oh, I love elevators!" I said. "Mom says I used to drive her plum crazy in Wheeling over riding the elevators. Mom has a terror of heights too."

"There, you see? People are born different. Some of those things we can't hack, doctors call phobias."

"Stone, is your stutter a phobia?"

"Petey!" Loni said.

Stone laughed his one-gun salute. "Oh, you noticed that, huh? Thought I had that licked. No, don't know. No rhyme or reason to it. I think it's more like hesitation. Just starting my engine."

Stone changed the subject right quick by suddenly pointing his finger at some quivering wintergreen down below.

A cottontail suddenly popped up and hightailed it through a tangle of budding sumac.

"I once saw a cottontail hopping over the trestle," I said. "If a dumb ol' rabbit can do it, why can't I? I got to learn."

"Shoot, and sometimes I got to take an elevator," Stone added. "I take a deep breath and pump air in and out of my lungs. That relaxes me a little. I even close my eyes and try to think of a vast landscape—moonlight on Lake Washington, anything free and open—and that helps."

"Stone, I can't close my eyes on that trestle, that's for sure."

"No siree," Stone grinned. He looked over at Loni, her tongue in the side of her mouth, struggling over her grid.

"That's the only dirty job I'll ask you to do, Loni," he called out.

"My lines aren't very straight," Loni said. "I hope you meant it when you said they dint—didn't—have to be."

"Nah," he nodded, "they get erased or covered over. Underlines agitate a drawing. Neat isn't always best."

"Now Pete," he said. I liked Stone calling me Pete, like I was grown up and all. "I've got a job for you too. You find a big long pole, a nice straight branch, I'd say this long." He stretched his arms as far as they could reach out.

"Longer than the bamboo. See, I think the problem was the bamboo pole was too light, too thin. Get something long enough to span that track bed, but heavy enough so your mind is worrying about holding the darn thing balanced. And you'll know that with that long, heavy pole, there is no way you can fall through that track bed."

"But there never was a way I could fall through. No way could I plunk through like greased lightning. It still don't make a matter. I freeze."

"No, it might not work. But here's how I figure it. The bigger pole will hide those spaces between the tracks."

So off I went, searching the woods for a clean pole. March winds had littered the leaves with a thicket of sticks and branches. Still, only one seemed close to right. I carried it back to tell Stone.

When I came 'round to the rock, Stone was kneeling aside Loni. They were squinting through the glass, his head pushed against hers, I guess to see it the way she was seeing. His free hand was over on her shoulder.

"Down in this corner...," he was saying to her as I came up to them.

Dad used to do that sometimes, get right over my shoulder and guide my hands as he knotted my tie or showed me how to make a letter. It mixed me up, seeing Loni letting Stone do the things Dad did.

"Hey," I said.

Stone kept on talking and pointing. Beside him was the pad he used to draw Loni. It was face down.

I turned it up.

It was boggling to see how Stone had edged in her eye patch. Almost like it wasn't there. It wasn't a blue patch at all, but sort of a blown-away outline.

"Hey, Loni," I said, "Stone did a neat picture of you."

That got Loni's attention.

"What?"

I held it up.

Loni jerked back from Stone. Her mouth formed something like "what?" again and hung open.

"Not too good." Stone handed it to Loni.

"All that time before, you were drawing me?" she finally said, shaking her head. "I never guessed."

"What do you think?" Stone asked.

"I don't allow pictures of me, I have to say that."

"That's fair. You don't have to keep it. I'll tear it up if you like, but as an artist, what do you think of it?"

"Oh heavens! I didn't mean that you should tear it up," Loni protested. "I was talking about snapshots with a Brownie camera. I don't think a person should ever tear up real art."

She stared into Stone's drawing like it was a looking glass. Nodded to fit her face inside that picture.

"I must say, it's the directest picture I ever say of anybody."

"Uh-huh," Stone said, waiting.

Close by, a thrush sounded—watery, like it had swallowed a song.

"It isn't finished, is it? I don't see how a body could get everything in so fast. I never could in a million years. But you dint—*didn't*—finish it did you? The patch and all?"

"The patch is there, isn't it," Stone said. "Didn't have to shout about it, did I? And who says everything has to be in a drawing. Artists have a license to put in and leave out anything they want. If I made that whole patch gray it would jump right out of the picture."

"Mom used to make her wear a white patch," I said, "but it got too dirty all the time. And it looked like a bandage. Then she made up some real pretty ones—"

"Petey," Loni broke in on me again. She turned to Stone. "It's none of anybody's beeswax about my eye."

"I w-wa-wasn't trying to hide it." Stone batted his eyes, trying to get *wasn't* out. "That patch is distinctive. Shoot, it's there. No need to be dishonest about it. I was thinking of the overall effect, too. A filled-in patch would distract from everything else."

"Yes, I guess it is distinctive," Loni said, allowing as though she always used a word I bet she never used before in her whole life. She tapped her patch like it was her buddy or something, but I knew better.

CHAPTER SIX

"N<small>oooooo</small>!" I twisted to free myself, but Olenk had a good grip on the back of my shirt.

"Come on, come on, sis," he said. "Walk the damn trestle." His fist was forced into my back. He gave me a shove and I stumbled over. My heel caught in a tie and I fell sideways, just flipped right over the side and—"Ahhhhhhhh..."

I woke up in a sweat. Mom's startled face was hanging over me like the moon, white, her mouth an O.

"The trestle?" Mom said. "Scares me to death. If we could afford any house that's out there—and there isn't any with this booming war—Petey, honest to God, I'd move in a day. I don't want you down there on that trestle at all. Wish I could walk it with you, but I'd die."

"But I got to learn. Year after next, Loni's off to Cokinville High, if she'll go. Then what?"

"Then we'll see. A lot can change in a year. War could be over or the short-haul buses could come back. But no matter, forget about the trestle. I don't want you on it, and that's that."

Later that morning, Loni took a while to dress.

Stone was letting us come see his studio. Said he'd help Loni with her drawings from nine to eleven Mondays and Wednesdays. He knew Mom didn't want Loni walking One-Mile Path alone, so he included me in.

Doors were slamming between her room and the bathroom. Mom finally went up, after Loni began yelling.

"Why do I have to do this?"

"Honey, do what you want! It was your idea."

"I'm ugly, I'm ugly, I'm just ugly."

"Honey, you're beautiful as the day. I wish I had your coloring and hair. You have your Dad's glowy Scotch-Irish skin. You look like you're wearing rouge. Your...ah...hazel eyes. A bunny-rabbit nose."

"Bunny-rabb— Oh, Mom." Loni's voice softened. Mom had a way. "I don't ever remember seeing a bunny-rabbit nose full of freckles."

"Honey, those freckles are just a tiny dusting-doo across the bridge of Waterloo. Like Toby. Cute."

"A little dusting-doo. Oh, gee, Mom."

"Honey, you can't expect to look like la-di-da Rita Hayworth at age fourteen. Although you're going to be as willow-right as she is. God's an artist, honey."

"Mom-ommmm," I heard Loni groan. "If God's an artist...well, I wish someone would tell me what he made freckles for. I mean when I paint a face, it's one color. I do not smear my brush in brown paint at the same time and let fly, speckling everything in sight. What kind of artist would that be, anyway?"

"One who plays hooky, honey. God helps those who help themselves with a dibbly-dash of makeup. And listen, honey, I mean to get serious now. If you'd only let us get your eye fitted. You know what Dr. Berdelli said. Sign of the cross and God rest his soul. You can't be putting that off. That socket can collapse. *Time* magazine itself says they now have a new plastic—"

"Mom, I'm not going to get a fake eye, glass or plastic. I feel like a freak as it is. And I don't have to go back to school, so I don't care how I look. The Queen of Halloween, that's me. There's nothing wrong with an eye patch, Stone says. So please let's not talk about it."

When Mom crossed over to my room, she whispered, "Geeszoy. Fiddle-faddle and double trouble, don't even say a word. She's wearing a dress."

Loni's white-and-brown saddle shoes were heavy on the stairs. I followed her down and studied the drawing she had finished the night before. It was spread out on the old dining room table.

"Real sneaky, using that eraser, Loni," I said. She had used an eraser to fake the steam rising off the creek. "It's real *real*-looking."

"Oh, you think so, Petey?" Loni said, now calm as cold mush. "I learned that watching Stone. It does two things. It gets the morning steam and blunks out some of my bad drawing of the trestle supports."

As we hiked One-Mile Path, Loni's stick whipped the daylights out of some of the overhanging briars. No weed would dare snare her dress that day.

All that fuss over a sun dress. Mom made it real pretty, though, blue with yellow flowers, guarded by a denim apron. She had a denim eye patch. Her long hair was tied back with a yellow ribbon that matched her dress.

I carried our drawings in Loni's satchel, so she was free to swing with both hands. She looked like my First Communion card of St. Michael Archangel, slaying the fallen.

"Petey," she said in a clearing uphill from Geeter's rock, "isn't it beautiful?" She pointed west to Catfish Pond. It was sparkling green, steaming fog. An old bachelor blue heron stood in its shallows like a stick.

Gen "No Trespass" Geeter's farm sat near the very top of Geeter hill, but in a little carve-out. You didn't dare walk on his property without phoning first. Otherwise, he'd scare the daylights out of you with a starting pistol and worse. Stray Cokinville kids never got the word, 'cause we could hear that gun going off right regular.

Mom called his house curlicue rose because of the lacy boards and spindles around the roof and porch. It was painted gray and trimmed in red. The porch looked out on a carriage house, a pond, grazing fields, meadows, and the valley beyond. White fences rode up and down and around like the tracks of a rolly-coaster, all seeming to run into the four corners of a big red barn. That's where Gen Geeter kept his Tennessee walkers.

"Just like to look at them," Gen often said.

"Yeah," Loni would whisper, "look, but don't touch. Won't even let us bring Toby up here on a lead."

He was sitting on his spindled porch in a high-back wicker chair, his marbled cigarette holder tilting up in his mouth like President Roosevelt in the Fox newsreels. His sandy hair stood right up like a crest. He'd make a good rooster for Walt Disney, the way he tilted his chin up, pointing his red beak nose to the roof.

We were glad Stone's studio was in the old carriage house on our side of his farm, so we didn't have to pass right smack in front of Gen Geeter's porch. But then Stone's deck entrance faced the side of Gen's porch, so Gen did see us whenever we visited Stone. It would be dumb to snub him. It was Gen who rented Mom our house after Dad died. He was sweet on her, but Mom finally cooled him off. Thank God. I didn't ever want to be called Peter Geeter.

"He's spying on us," I whispered to Loni, as we waved.

"Shhhh, he'll hear you."

Stone was sitting outside on his deck rail, waiting for us with a coffee mug in his hand. He looked pleased when he saw Loni. He didn't say a word about her dress, either. It was the drawing he latched on to.

"Loni, that's A-one!" he said. He set his cup on the rail and slapped the drawing down on the deck. He gave it a long, staring look. Then stood right up and gave Loni a big hug.

Loni's face lit up like lightning flashed over it. The whole time after, her hands kept brushing her hair into the bow. I knew she was about as happy as she could be.

I didn't think I'd ever get a hug for anything I did.

Drawing wasn't my strong suit. I mean I could never make things *real*. But Stone said a writer for Walt Disney didn't have to know how to draw. What counted was that my drawings were very expressive. Expressive was his word. Sometimes they came out so expressive they were plain cockeyed. Then Stone and Loni would bust out laughing.

"I didn't mean that FHF fighter to be funny," I said about the airplane I copied for my Wednesday drawing.

"I can see that, Pete," Stone said. He slapped a sheet of see-through paper over it and lined up the wings with a pencil.

"Now it's accurate. But bor-ing," he said. Then he whisked the see-through away. Admit it. Isn't it fun to see a drawing that hasn't been through basic training?"

"Mmmm," Loni said, changing the subject, "it smells so nice in here."

"That's your oak. I just put the whole shebang in." Stone waved his arm to the cabinets and sink that went down one side of the big open room.

Beside the sink were two burners, mugs, and a speckled blue coffee pot set on a while oilcloth.

"That's the mess. All I need. I eat up in Cokinville a lot."

Pointing to a daybed with a quilt thrown over it, he said, "That's my bunk. There's a shower and latrine out back. It was for hired help.

"They finally hooked up that phone. It's a party line, though." He pointed to a divider with a flat metal radio aside the kitchen things. "Now I'm all set for the summer."

That day and the next Wednesday, we got to know Stone real well.

Mom often said I shouldn't ask "persnickety-blue" personal questions, and Loni said that if I did ask questions I should be nonchalant. Here we were with nonchalant again. Pretending it was nothing special. It seemed dumb. If you were pretending, then you were really caring. That would be being chalant, not nonchalant, but Loni said her dictionary had no such word as chalant.

"Stone," I said, trying to yawn nonchalant, "what year were you born in?"

I thought that was a nicer way of asking a grown-up his age than coming right out and saying "Hey, how old are you anyway?"

Stone didn't flinch one bit.

"I was born in nineteen-fifteen," he said. "I'm twenty-nine."

Now that's what I call decent. He didn't even leave it to me to do the subtracting. Whenever I asked Miss Roaster, or one of my teachers, how old they were, I'd always get a twisted mouth-pursing face and this song and dance: "Well, Peter, how old do you think I am?"

I honestly believe that is the worst, rottenest, sneakiest way to get back at a kid. So I stopped asking, even if

I hurt their feelings by not asking. I always came up with the wrong answer, anyhow. The problem was Mom looked so young for her age, and that's what I had to go on. From the stretched-face looks teachers threw at me, my guess was usually way too old. That never set well for your grade if it was hanging on the edge of a minus.

"You shouldn't have asked Stone's age," Loni said on our way home.

"I didn't," I said. "I asked what year he was born in."

"That's the same thing. And don't tell Mom."

"Why not?"

"Because Mom's older, thirty-one, and that will rub it in."

I didn't say so to Loni, but I guess I needed to rub it in.

I said, "I think she'd feel good she's not that much older." I tapped out the years on my fingers. "Three years. Whew. I guess that is a lot."

"It is not," Loni said. "And don't you ever say that to Mom."

"Listen, don't you care about Dad at all?"

"What does Dad have to do with it?"

"I mean you act like you want Mom to marry Stone."

"I never said that. I just want Mom to go out."

"You didn't act that way when Gen Geeter asked her out. You did a lot of stomping around."

"So did you if I remember kee-rectly, and I do."

Loni put her nose in the air and did a good imitation of No-Kids-No-Trespass Geeter growling at us: "Stay out of the barn, away from the oil well, don't be pulling up things, and don't walk the fences. No dogs—that stray Toby you have."

I laughed. Calling Toby a stray as he did—even if he was—was like calling Gen's Lincoln a jalopy.

Loni said, "I know Mom likes Stone."

"Sure, I like Stone, but Mom doesn't like his beard, and he stutters."

"He got that in the war, Petey. He's getting over it. You've said that."

"I guess. I just don't like Mom being someone's girl friend."

"Gosh sakes, it's just for dinner. Do you really think Dad would want Mom to have no friends? Do you?"

"I don't know. I don't know what Dad would think about anything anymore. He's dead and never ever coming back."

"Oh, Petey!"

CHAPTER SEVEN

Stone was letting Loni and me come up for an extra morning of lessons! Right from the first week, we got to come up Thursday as well as Monday and Wednesday.

"I hope you two didn't wheedle-loo that," Mom said.

"It was his idea, Mom," Loni said. "He liked my drawing real well."

Loni went on, her hand fluttering down over her hair. "Don't you think he's nice-looking, Mom?"

"I can't tell much with that whiskery beard," Mom said.

"Oh, I like it now," Loni said. "It's real distinguished-looking. Artists should look distinguished. Even Stone says so himself."

"Well, geeszoy," Mom said, "I better start thinking of how la-di-da distinguished I better look when he and his buddy come for dinner."

Stone was out near the horse corral with Gen Geeter when we showed up. We waved and sat on the rail, leaning out to see what was new in the clearing behind the carriage house. Gen Geeter's handyman used it to burn off gunk from tractor parts he was always fixing.

Sure enough, in a charred circle set off by white-washed stones was an engine block.

"I wonder how much money Junk John would pay us for that," Loni said to me.

"Count me out," I said, remembering the last time we collected junk on Gen's property.

"The old skinflint," Loni said.

I had other business to think about. "We got to find out how Mom should dress when Stone comes for dinner," I said.

"No we don't," Loni said. "And I hope you're not trying to embarrass him into dressing up."

"I'm not. I decided it's okay for Mom to invite him to dinner."

"That's real George of you, Petey. Real George!"

I saw my chance when Stone came in. He sat on the daybed and shucked off his muddy cowboy boots. They were his prewar Washington state boots, all scuffed and just beautiful the way they were fancy tooled. They seemed bigger than Dad's shoes, but Stone's feet were smaller in socks. Right there, I gave Dad a higher grade for feet.

I popped up my eyebrows at Loni.

"Is it possible to dress up in cowboy boots?" I asked, my voice so nonchalant Stone asked me to repeat it. That about ruined it. Loud ruins nonchalant. But Stone was his usual flat-out self.

"Sure," he grinned, lining up his boots and setting them down. "At hoedowns, they're what you want."

"To dinner out?" I asked, not too nonchalant, I guessed, because Loni about fell off the ice cream chair.

Stone laughed, his two-grunt salute. He was putting

his bare feet into moccasins. I wondered if he were part Indian. He was so tan and leathery he could pass for one.

'No, not these old pals."

The game was almost up, but I wasn't going to come right out and ask what Mom should wear.

"So then will you wear your moccasins?"

"Nah, Pete," Stone said, grinning. "I'll polish up my old dress shoes."

"So there," I said to Loni as we headed down One-Mile Path. "Now we can tell Mom it's dressy."

Loni grabbed my arm and pulled me over. Something was rustling along in the sumacs and thickets beside the path.

"Keep walking," she whispered. "Act like we're just talking."

Off to the side, I caught glimpses of blue cloth sliding in and out of the heavy brush and trees.

"It's Olenk," Loni whispered. "Play-act."

She stepped out smartly in front of me, slapping a menacing stick against some exposed oak roots and shouting, "GEE WASN'T IT GREAT THAT GEN GEETER UP ON THE HILL GAVE US THAT ENGINE BLOCK. I BET WE GET FIVE DOLLARS EASY FOR THAT FROM JUNK JOHN."

"EASY," I shouted, not knowing what Loni wanted me to say.

"BUT WE BETTER GET HOME AND CHANGE CLOTHES. MR. GEETER SAID WE GOT TO HAUL THAT ENGINE BLOCK DOWN

FROM BEHIND THE CARRIAGE HOUSE BEFORE HE GIVES IT TO
SOMEONE ELSE."

"WE BETTER," I said.

"GEN GEETER SAID HE WANTED IT OUT OF THERE BEFORE
LUNCH, SO LET'S RUN PETEY.."

Then Loni smacked the trunk of a maple, and off we
ran, down One-Mile Path to home.

As Mom was setting our toasted cheese sandwiches
before us, we heard the sharp crack-crack of No
Trespass's starting pistol going off.

"Uh-oh," Mom said, "someone trespassing up there.
He better know how to run before Gen Geeter's buck-
shot comes out. He'll get his potatoes peppered with a
little onion on the side."

"Yeah," Loni said, "I wonder who'd be dumb enough
to poach No Trespass's stuff in broad daylight."

"I wonder," Mom said, raising her eyebrows. She
meant the time Loni and me dug up a huge toothed
piece of metal in Gen's woods. We just about got twin
hernias lugging it home.

Loni was figgering up how much we'd make on it—
about enough to buy Mom a mink coat, she figgered—
when Gen rolled down in his yellow convertible. His arm
was hooked over the Lincoln's sleeked-up door, his beak
nose in the air.

"We dug it up, Mr. Geeter," Loni said. "It wasn't on
top of the ground."

"It was curing," Gen said and winked at Mom. "The Cosmoline gunk."

I didn't know why he winked, unless he was lying. "It's for the war effort, Mr. Geeter. We collect scrap for the war effort."

"You sell it to Junk John, don't you?"

"Yes, sir," I said. "But he sells it to the war effort."

"Kids," Mom interrupted, "put that in Gen's car and apologize right this minute."

"Sorry, Ali," he said, opening his trunk, "parts are scarce. No hard feelings."

We lugged it to the car and mumbled apologies. What could we do? He owned the whole hill; our house, too. He could raise the rent on Mom in a minute.

When he drove off, I yelled, "But it was for the war effort, Mr Geeter...Sir."

"I hope you both learned a lesson from that time," Mom said.

We both covered our mouths before we told Mom about how Loni tricked Olenk.

"Well," Mom said, "I guess we won't see that Olenk trestling around here anymore."

CHAPTER EIGHT

"Stone has a new number," Mom said. "But it won't give him any more privacy, I expect. 9-J's the number, not 9-K, and he's on Gen Geeter's line. I believe it's the only line up there, so I guess Gen can put his ear to it any time."

"Did he say they were coming, Mom?" Loni sounded worried.

"Yes," Mom said. "We had a nice stop-and-go talk. He said the phone makes him stutter more and apologized all over the switchboards. I said I didn't stand still for the King's English myself, so he could stutter away."

"But when is he coming, Mom?"

"He—*they're* coming for dinner Sunday. Stone has to drive over to Pittsburgh tomorrow. He's getting treatment at the Veterans Hospital. And he's bringing a friend back. So there won't be any lessons maybe for a few days."

"What's he getting treated for?" I wanted to know.

"He didn't say, and we shouldn't ask. He's worn down, for one thing. Looks like a laid-off scarecrow, for another, and that stutter means something. He said you should keep drawing, Loni."

"I wish he was coming alone," said Loni.

"Oh, honey," Mom said, "all those boys could use a home-cooked meal with a few whistles on the side."

"Whistles on the side, Mom?" I usually didn't ask

about Mom's expressions. They were usually just free-run.

"Whisky," Mom said, winking at me.

"Sh-shoot," I said, imitating Stone.

"I think he's trying not to use swear words with that 'shoot.' Now, kids, I'll need some help. Denny Dorfapple and the Brown's van will be here anytime. I'll pick up the groceries we need.

"Petey, that porch needs a mop. Loni, I'd appreciate your sweeping and dusting the rugs, but make sure you cover your eye."

Mom waited for Loni's usual protest about wearing her eye patch at home, but she nodded, looking glum about something. Not housework. She was a real help to Mom there.

"Then there's the floors. I'll help you with those as soon as I get back, although I'll have to do the pies. Too early for apples. I'll have to get canned pumpkin. That's not rationed or short in June, I don't believe."

Our—Gen Geeter's—rambling house came down in steps from a wooded hillside. Mom's and Loni's back bedrooms were over the kitchen and the roof of a sitting porch out back. Out front, wide battleship-gray wooden steps climbed to a long front porch.

Gen Geeter kept the house spruce and painted the color of his, gray and red. But it never looked spruce. We were under a tent of trees, mostly locust, buried in blossoms, seed pods, falling apples, or leaves the year round. You would think the porch roof would keep that porch clear, but what with stuff blowing in from the sides, Toby dancing 'round with muddy paws, and the grit blowing up from all those troop trains down below, it was always in need of sweeping and mopping.

That was my job. I swept the loose stuff off. Got a pail of water from the side spigot, added some Rinso, and sloshed it down with the mop. Hosed the soap suds off. Rinsed and wrung-out the mop and sopped up the puddles. I set a wicker chair against the front door so no one would track it until it was dry.

We tied Toby up in back until the porch dried off. He was a house dog but didn't know it. Bred to be a birder, his soft, freckled jowls were like velvet. Turned loose, we feared he'd head for the river and get lost.

Dad took him hunting when we lived nearer Cokinville. But we couldn't.

"Poor Toby," Mom said after Dad died, "no hunting, but lots of love." Toby jumped up on her lap and tried to lick her tears. *You have me, baby.*

Loni didn't want him underfoot, either. She was cleaning and waxing the linoleum.

When Mom got back, she had a surprise. Two gold frames!

"Not one decent frame at Murphy's Five and Dime," Mom said. "Had to go to Jon's Photo Shop. He gets priority because he does servicemen, or so he sings. I bet he got them on the black market; they were dear enough."

"Oh, Mom, that's great," Loni said, grabbing them

and running upstairs to put in the drawings. Then she got nails and a hammer.

"Wait a minute, honey," Mom said. "I don't want traveling nail holes in the new wallpaper 'til we're sure. Let's just set them on their stands on the side buffet."

By four o'clock, Toby had a bath and was lying in the dining room on a towel, pouting. As I moved in on him with a hair brush, he started growling. *I'll eat you alive, I will.*

Didn't mean a thing.

"Growl away," I said as I brushed him. His great white chest was blinding, it was so clean. The black patches and speckles on his hindquarters shone like they'd been greased with brilliantine. His long ears kinked in curls. Oh, he was so pretty Mom said she could cry just looking at him.

"Shame on you, growling at Petey," she said, looking 'round the kitchen door to admire him. She had the pumpkin pies out of the oven, and the house smelled like spice heaven. "Shame. Pooty-poo."

Toby gulped, gulped, ducked his head like Lou Costello, the comic, and rolled his moist, sad eyes up at Mom. *I'm just a baaaaaad boy.*

"Oh, yes," Mom said, petting him, "we know, oh don't we know.

Mom sighed. "Now all we have to do is spruce ourselves up in the morning like Calypso kings and queens and set the table."

CHAPTER NINE

Loni's door was closed.

"Loni, honey," Mom said through the door, "Stone and his friend will be here any minute. I can use some help."

"The table's all set, Mom." Loni's hushed voice came through the door.

"Honey, you will come down?"

"I'll see."

"Oh land, geeszoy, and double trouble," Mom whispered to me on the landing. "This is what Dr. Berdelli I guess was hinting at. Stone just brought her right out, but with anyone else now it's back in her shell."

At noon on the stroke, Stone pulled up in the brown Chevy woody wagon lent to him by Cokin Steel. Loni was still upstairs.

I waited outside the front screen door with Toby on a leash. Mom, just inside, gasped when she saw the young Marine angle out of the front seat. The sun glanced a blinding shot off something in his right hand. Well, it wasn't his right *hand*. It was a steel claw. He had thrown off his jacket and tie, but his open khaki shirt had corporal's stripes.

Mom whispered from behind the screen door, "Oh dear and die. He's just a boy."

Yes. If I ever wrote him up for Walt Disney, I'd have

to make him something like maybe a pup or a colt. His black hair was crew cut. His pale face looked scrubbed with a brush that left one wide pink smear down each cheek. Like he was blushing. But in truth he wasn't a bit bashful.

"I'm Boone Barone," he said, after bounding up the stairs. He offered his left hand.

I tried not to stare at his claw, even look at it, knowing how much that hurt Loni when people stared at her. But it was hard not to, the way he prided about it.

"Now watch this," he said, in the living room, holding his claw up in the air. "I got this down so I can pick up a peanut."

Sure enough, he pinched a nut from our World's Fair, bowl as quick as a crow. Then he shifted it to his good hand, threw it up in the air, and caught it in his mouth.

Toby sat up and begged. Bounced his crossed paws, barked. *Cripe's sakes, Pal, we're not talking steak.*

I took his collar and pulled him into the sewing room. He flopped down like a wet mop, snout flat on the floor, and snorted in disgust.

"I'll bring you something good, Toby."
Snort.

When I returned, Mom was saying to Boone, "Loni's a little shy. I don't know if we can coax her down for dinner."

Stone winked at Mom. Said, "Pete, I have to wash

my hands. Can you lead the way?" He tramped up the stairs, whistling "Tangerine." Loni would hear that.

I followed after, hovering on the landing.

When Stone came out of the bathroom, I pointed to Loni's door. Stone stood close by and said, "Whataya drawing, Loni? Can I see?"

That brought Loni out fast—and down.

After dinner, Boone said to Loni, "Stone says you do great comics. Can I see them?"

"Oh," Loni hesitated.

"Sure," Stone said.

"Why don't you take Boone upstairs and show him," Mom said. "You too, Petey. And get His Royal Highness."

I figgered she wanted to talk about something private with Stone, so I let Toby out of the sewing room and we followed after, his nails clicking too loud.

I stopped him on the stairs to check his feathery paws.

He chuffed and pulled. *Don't even think about cutting my nails.*

In Loni's room, Boone was studying her comics with a locked-in stare like Stone's. Even holding them up in the air and flipping them sideways in the light. Strange. He was putting a little too much show on it, and then he did something even more strange. He leaned from his chair, facing Loni on the bed, pushed his face right up to hers and said, "Loni, do you see anything peculiar about my face?"

Loni drew back, puzzled. "Peculiar? Like what?"

"This eye?" he said, pointing to his right eye, which as far as I could see was the same blue color as his left.

Loni tilted her head. "I—"

"It's fake, Loni," Boone said.

"Fake?"

"It's plastic, Loni."

Loni put her hand over her mouth.

"Oh. Ohhhhh..."

"Yes, it's one of the new plastic eyes. Mine took shrapnel on Roi Island in the Marshalls. A sliver. It didn't touch my face. But eventually they had to enucleate— take it out."

Loni turned her head, squinting at his eye with her own good eye. It was like she didn't believe him.

"I'll show you. Is there a bathroom up here?"

I led the way, I was almost stumbling I was so excited. In the bathroom, Boone stood aside the looking glass and cupped a towel over his hooked hand. He then reached into his trousers pocket and pulled out a little plastic cup. Then he lowered his head over the towel, placed the cup over his eye, pulled it away, and then turned the cup over the towel.

There it was, upside down, looking like a clam shell or one of the gnocchi noodles Mom made by pressing her thumb in a little circle of dough.

He then went to the washbasin, rinsed the fake eye, dried it, and held it out to us. It was an eye all right.

Right in the middle of the white shell. The shell even had little red veins in it.

In a minute, before the looking glass, he forced the eye back in. Then he craned at Loni, opened his eyes wide, and gave her a big goofy smile.

CHAPTER TEN

The morning after Boone had dinner with us, Loni got a tad peevish at breakfast. She said to Mom, "Whose idea was that?"

"Idea to do what?" Mom said, nonchalant, looking down at a wiggle of sunlight that was trying to dance into her coffee cup. She liked to serve us breakfast in the dining room near the big window. Outside our back screen door, a blue jay was scolding something, maybe a stray cat.

"Mom-om." Loni crossed her arms and frowned. "To invite Boone Barone."

"I'll be dead honest," Mom said, running a finger along her brow, like she was coaxing her brain. "Stone told me about Boone when I invited him to dinner. He knows a lot of the vets getting treatment in Pittsburgh."

"You mean he just accidentally ran into him."

"Honey, Stone cares about you. He went to the eye clinic and inquired right and left. Boone was there. Is that so bad?"

"No, I didn't mean tha-at," Loni said after staring into her bowl of Grape Nuts a second. "But it dint—*didn't*— have to be such a surprise, did it? You could have told me before Boone came that he had a glass—plastic—eye."

"If you were invited to dinner, would you like the hostess lady to tell her guests that you had a plastic eye?

Oh, geeszoy, all right, we wanted you to be...wool-outed."

"I certainly was wool-outed," I said, wondering where Mom got *that* word.

Outside, the blue jay began to sound like a strangling cricket.

"Wool-outed," Loni said, sighing. "But I wonder, I have to wonder, how much of a normal person this Boone is. It doesn't mean everybody who gets a plastic eye will look that normal."

"That bird!" Mom said. "Is Toby out there?"

"Mom-om," Loni said. "He's in the kitchen. Mom, I'm talking to you. Forget that dumb bird."

"Honey, I'm sorry, I'm all addlepated."

"What I mean is, why do I have to look normal? Why does anybody care how I look? Stone said I looked distinctive with a patch. Said I dint—didn't—need to be dishonest. Said I had a real talent in art. Then he turns right around and tries to trick me into getting a plastic eye. He's just like everybody else. Nobody cares *who* I am. It's always what I look like that matters. Well, they can all go jump in Logan Creek. I don't need people. They can all drown for all I care."

Loni spun 'round and dashed down the hall to the stairs.

"I don't think it's the eye," Mom said. "I think she's sore afraid of what it may take to get an eye. I really do. All that time at Wheeling General, trussed up, face bandaged, and Dad gone. Oh, I wish..."

"Boone said his operation was easy as winking."

"We'll keep kitty-catting her that," Mom said.

At lunchtime, Loni came back down. Said she wasn't hungry. I think she felt bad storming out on Mom but couldn't say it.

Mom took a deep breath. "Honey, don't get upset now." She patted Loni's shoulder. "I called Stone. He said he already made that darn appointment. I didn't know what to tell him."

"Tell him to go jump in Logan Creek."

CHAPTER ELEVEN

"Mom, Loni's closed the door on her room again. I told her Stone was in the drive, we were waiting, but she didn't answer."

"Oh, dear. Petey, I'm half-dressed. Her door won't lock, so just go right in and see what the trouble is."

I eased Loni's door open a peek.

"Go away."

"Loni, Stone's here."

"I know that."

I walked in. She was dressed but propped up on her bed, looking like a scared baby bird in a big nest. Her blue eye patch was pulled up onto her forehead. Her bad eye was red and angry, her good one tearful. Her old yellowing Motorola sat still, hushing me down to a whisper.

"Hey, Loni," I said real soft. "Hey, Loni."

"Yeah."

"Dad would want to you to do this."

"Dad's gone."

"Hey, Loni. You know what you said to me about crossing the trestle? You know how fearful it makes me. But when I said to Stone I wish there was a wizard like in *The Wizard of Oz*, you said the wizard was a humbug. Well, I looked it up in your book. And you're right."

"What's that got to do with a hill of beans?"

"Well..."

"Well?"

"The idea is that to be brave you still got to try even if you're afraid. You're ten times braver than me, Loni. And I'm trying to cross that damn—darn—trestle."

"I am *not* afraid, Pe—" She began to cry. Just shook, crying, her scrubbed pink fingers atremble.

In the movies, Clark Gable always handed the leading lady his hankie when she cried. So I did the same, handing over my dress-up hankie. It was Dad's, with a blue P initial, my favorite. But I didn't want her to actually use it, so I slid over her bedside box of Kleenex. She took a tissue but held onto my hankie.

"Okay," she said finally, tapping her eye patch. "I'll tell you just exactly what I'm thinking. You know how I used to hate wearing this patch. Dint wear it most of the time. Sometimes just to be ornery. To make kids stare and gag. To get back at kids that made remarks. Well, Stone made me real proud of this patch. It was like...like"—Loni held up her hands and looked 'round the room. Her eye settled on the ribbons she had won for her art.—"a big prize ribbon right on my face. I promised God I would never, never rile anyone with my eye anymore. Honest, Petey, I did. I would wear Mom's best patches like prize ribbons, and just be real rocking proud, Petey. And never, never let anyone see me without it. My bad eye would be my special secret self."

Loni scrubbed her eyes with another Kleenex, looked to her left and right to make sure no one else had sneaked into the room, and took a big breath.

"Stone is a traitor," she whispered.

"He wants to help you, Loni."

"He *was* helping me. He *was*! He dint have to get me a plastic eye to do it! Petey, do you know what they make out of plastic? False teeth! Out of plastic. Uggle!"

"But, Loni," I said, "think. You don't have to give up your patch. With a plastic eye, you can have two ways of looking. You could still wear your patch over your fake eye if you wanted. You could really be the mean Queen of Halloween any time you pleased."

"Mean Queen of Halloween. Oh, boy." she smiled, taking Dad's good hankie and—cripe's sakes!—wiping her whole nose with it.

"Petey, you're a screwball, you know that?"

"Yeah, but do you mind just using the Kleenex? That hankie was for Pittsburgh."

"Oh. Oh, I'm sorry," Loni smoothed the hankie out on the bed and refolded it. Then she slapped it down, but it bounced up and flip-flopped in the air on its starched, springy creases, which made us both bust out laughing.

"You coming down now?" I said, getting my breath.

"Okay, okay, I'll be down. But listen, buster." She snarled like a Dead End Kid. "Nobody's going to make me wear it, see?"

CHAPTER TWELVE

Stone drove us over Route 22 to Pittsburgh, to the Children's Free Eye Clinic.

Cokin Steel mill let him have free use of the X sticker on their brown Chevy woody wagon, which meant he could get as much gas as he wanted. The wagon was too loose sprung to be the Ghost Car and not the right type or color, although I wouldn't mind Stone being the one if there had to be a stand-in ghost for Dad.

I noticed he was shifting a wooden knob on the gear handle under the steering wheel. It was new wood, and I wondered if Stone had tooled it himself.

I was about to tell him if he ever got his hands on an old gear-shift knob shaped like a skull, I'd save up my junk money to buy it. But since Loni was in such a state, I decided I'd best shut up about things like skulls. There was too much talking about doctors and clinics as it was

Mom was curious about the Navy doctor who set up the free clinic. "Hard to believe a dentist would work on eyes," she said.

"Strange, isn't it? Boony says they were already working with molding plastics, false teeth and such."

"You call him Boony?" I yelled from the back seat.

"Ol' Boony. Only to tease. His father liked Daniel—ah—Boone, and that's how he got that name."

Ol' Boony. Loni rolled her eyes, acting disgusted. She

wasn't too happy with Boony, either. It was Boony who talked to Commander Soliti about Loni before Stone called.

At dinner the other night, Boony told us that Commander Soliti was not really an eye doctor, but a Navy dentist on tee-dee-wye—that meant leave—to the vets hospital. According to Boony, it was the Navy dentists who came up with the plastic eye. They got the idea from a dentist in Africa, and got clicking on it when the vets hospitals started running out of glass eyes. By March this year they fitted their first plastic eye.

"Commander Soliti is from around here," Stone said as we got near Pittsburgh.

Soon, the spans of Point Bridge were clicking by us. The Monongahela was dark as molasses under us, the Triangle dead ahead. Stop lights and neon signs cut through the darkness. The air smelled of sulfur.

"Geeszoy," Mom said, holding up her wristwatch. "It's eleven in the morning and you'd think it was eight-at-the-stroke at night."

"The mills are working 'round the clock," Stone said. "Blast furnaces pouring it out."

"I thought Cokinville was bad. How do people live here?"

Stone sang, "'Oh give me a home where the buffalo roam, where the deer and the antelope play...'" It was perfect. I thought maybe he should try singing all his words.

"God, how I miss the West."

"Stone," Mom said, "I never asked how you landed here. Well, maybe I shouldn't ask."

"No, no. It's a funny story. *Life* magazine did a story on G.I. art. Picked one of my hospital paintings."

Stone batted his eyes, surprised like Gary Cooper in the movies. I expected he'd say his favorite word, *shoot*, but he didn't.

He went on. "Bob Feller, who runs Cokin Steel, saw my painting. Called me up and asked if I'd like to do a mural. Gave me the use of the Chevy wagon, unlimited gas stamp and all. Found me this place. I m-m-m-made a deal with Gen Geeter: I'd fix it up for the rent."

Stone laughed. "'Course I didn't know how much fixing up he wanted me to do. 'Bout near rebuilt the whole thing. Bob Feller got me the varnish and lent me tools. Gen Geeter was hoarding a barnful of lumber."

"Bob Feller's an arrow-straight man," Mom said. "He came dressed like royalty to the house, before and after Pete's funeral. My husband—Pete—supervised the coke plant at Cokin Steel. Bob Feller has never dropped us from one diddly mill benefit. Not one. He never forgets a name, they say, and mind you, I know he doesn't."

Mom got real quiet. I thought she was going to cry.

"When this war is all over, Stone," she said finally, "I'm going to learn to drive, get in a car, and not stop until I see the sun set in California, I swear."

"I'll teach you to drive, Alita, if you really mean it."

Mom shrugged. "That's just it. Do I really mean a fig

about it, Stone? I guess it must be the car accident that makes me back off when I get a chance to learn."

"Shouldn't berate yourself about it. But I'm ready when you are."

I didn't say it, but Pittsburgh was my favorite place. Dad used to drive us over to the dinosaur museum when we were little. As we neared the city, Dad would say, "Here comes Pittsburgh, the big snorting dragon, belching smoke and fire, stinking of sulfur, rattling over its iron bridges, look out, look out, kids."

"Pete, you're going to give them nightmares," Mom would say. And it did—the best nightmares I ever had.

Stone was saying, "Before Pearl Harbor, the city set up a co-committee to try to control the smoke, but the war got in the way."

"It's a wonder you can see your way around, Stone," Mom said, craning her neck. "I can't tell the street signs from shop neon lights. What I *can* see are so grim-grimy I can't read them."

"I know my way now. The clinic is up the river a ways, in Aspinwall, a bit south of the vets hospital. The air's a little better out there."

The clinic was in a gray stone, churchlike building with arched doors. Stone left us off at the door, promising he'd be parked nearby before we were through. He gave Loni a troubled look before he left, but she kept her head down. I saw his Adam's apple working up and down. I guess he was swallowing whatever he wanted to say.

We entered into a big high-ceiling place that looked even more like a church. The stone walls were lined with little pointy-headed frames of people with their insides showing.

But—oh joy!—ahead of us was an elevator.

An old black man in a gray uniform with gold braid dragged open the crisscross green metal doors, sang out the floors, and rattled us up to my breathless heaven.

Commander Soliti let us in himself. Now, let's see...yeah. If he was a character in Walt Disney, I'd make him a Scotty. He was short and dark. His hair was cut short, black and wiry, and he had real thick, shaggy, Scotty eyebrows. Too bad he wasn't wearing a plaid sweater. Instead, he wore a white smock with a name tag, white pants, and shoes caked with white shoe polish.

"You're my only schedule today, Mrs. Burns. Let's see, this must be Loni."

We weren't in a waiting room, but directly in his workshop. White counters, cabinets, and sinks ringed the room. There was a slanted drawing board at the far end with sideboard tables. Tubes of paints and brushes in glasses were on the tables. White paper was tacked to the drawing board all raring to go. It smelled a little like Stone's studio, the turpentine and all. I wondered if Commander Soliti was an artist too.

"Petey, if you want, you can go through that door and read," Commander Soliti said. "Some good *National Geographics* in there. We're at the far end of the clinic here. Dr. Mundell will be in shortly."

I searched through every *National Geographic* in the room for the animal photographs. But what stopped me awhile was a torn-up piece on some Pacific island before the war, native women naked right down to the belly button and beads and not caring. Since they didn't care, they looked more decent than the Kleenex ladies, sniffling in pert-near see-through nightgowns, that the other magazines carried as ads.

When Mom and Loni came out, Loni was pouting. Mom had a worried look on her face.

"What happened?" I asked as we went down in the elevator.

"They want me to have another operation," Loni whispered, making a sorrowful face.

Stone was waiting out front, standing at the Chevy. As we pulled out, Mom explained to Stone what Dr. Mundell had told her.

"They said it wasn't a good idea for us to fiddle any longer. He wants to put in an implant, one that will actually allow her artificial eye to just move natural. Commander Soliti says we shouldn't worry one iota about the cost. He says his is a free clinic, and he's pretty sure Pete's Cokin Steel plan will pick up Dr. Mundell's fee, as they did at Wheeling Hospital."

Loni finally spoke up. She hadn't said one word to Stone the whole trip.

"A patch is distinctive," she said. "Stone, you said

that. I don't have to follow the crowd and go through with this, do I?"

Stone cleared his throat, "Ah, L-Loni, you're right, and I'd say st-stick by the patch, but only if something else couldn't be done. Nobody likes to be stared at a-all their lives. You'll want your privacy, to be anonymous in a crowd, if you can have it."

"I know it's upsetting, honey," Mom said. "But Dr. Mundell says he doubts it will take longer than three to four weeks to heal."

"I know, Mom," Loni said, her head down.

"It's just a short stay," Mom added.

"Will I be able to learn to paint, Stone?" Loni asked, coloring up a bit.

"Shoot, you'll only have a bandage over one eye."

"Listen," Mom said, "I was worried about your using your eye so much, and asked Dr. Mundell about it right out. He said that you're in no more danger of eyestrain than a person with two good eyes."

Stone took us to a cafeteria on Forbes Street, near the Carnegie Institute. Afterward, he said he had a surprise for us.

As soon as I saw the great gray building with black statues hovering on the roof, the Carnegie Museum, I knew we were going to see the dinosaur skeletons.

"But not right away," Stone said.

He led us past two seated bronze figures, one Michelangelo and the other Galileo, up flights of stairs, into a cool marble entry, then up to the second floor to a room filled with paintings. There, he led us over to a special painting called *Young Woman Picking Fruit*. The painting was of a lady in a kind of bluish pink dress reaching up into the frame, picking a pear. In front of her was another lady in a blue flowery dress and black hat, looking up at her.

"I wanted you to see this, Loni," Stone said, speaking very slowly, and almost without a stutter.

"It's by Mary Cassatt, who was born in Pittsburgh. She had a difficult time being accepted as a painter. Left the country and went to France to live and paint. She had beat-all faith in her talent. What do you think?"

Loni tilted her head, reading the label, brushing at her hair.

"Mary Cassatt," she repeated. "I like the painting, but why does she push everyone to the left side? I mean, the seated lady is cut off, and the lady picking the pear has her hand cut off. There's enough room over here on the right side to put them in the center."

"It was a different way of looking," Stone said, still real slow. "Less formal. More natural, like a photograph. Gives a more spontaneous feeling. Also, sometimes you want to push things off center, balance the painting in a fresh way."

Loni nodded, tilting her head this way and that.

Stone went on about Mary Cassatt. You could see right there, Stone was going to be a teacher. He was all hepped up about that painting and wanted to talk about it without a stutter. And just about did too.

"Actually," he said, "Mary Cassatt did a lot of studies and paintings of women or children picking fruit. She did a mural about the same time. She called it young women picking the fruit of knowledge—something like that—handing the fruit down to children. So this idea intrigued her. She was struggling to make something of her art, and in a sense was encouraging women to make something of themselves."

Mom went up real close to the painting, studying the blue dress with the flowers.

"Up close, they're as free as loose thread," Mom said of the flowers. "But back there, I really saw them as hard embroidery."

"You know, Alita, one of her artist friends, Degas—you've probably seen reproductions of his ballet dancers—when he saw this painting, said, 'No woman has a right to draw like that.' Which says something about what she was up against even when she was praised."

Stone took us around to other paintings. Showing us how different artists looked at things in different ways. It got kind of boring for me. When I yawned, Stone said, "Okay, Pete says it's time to see the dinosaurs."

The dinosaurs were downstairs. Mom's heels clicked over red, gray, and white marble floors as we moved through a high room with white statues of naked Greek men and clothed ladies standing under a glass ceiling. It was very embarrassing.

Finally, we entered a long hall.

And there they were, the dinosaurs, looking like the bones of giant chickens, except they had big heads with sharklike teeth. I'd forgotten that they weren't white at all, but oily and smoky like they had been left out in the Pittsburgh air too long. As we walked under them, I had to smile, thinking of Dad. He used to say, "Look out kids, it's raining down bones."

At the end of the hall, *Tyrannosaurus rex* towered over us, ready to clamp down his dagger teeth. The sign said he was one of only two complete skeletons in existence, and he weighed seven tons. I guessed that was before he was stripped to the gears.

"Hard to believe," Stone said.

"These things always give me the shivery-shakes," Mom said. "You wonder if someone made them up out of a bone nightmare."

"They would be hard to draw," Loni said. "So many lines. It would be hard to tell one bone from the other."

"They give you some of the same problems as the trestle four-by-fours," Stone said.

Later, going home in the Chevy, Loni said, "Stone, I was thinking about Mary Cassatt. I'm going to pick from the tree of knowledge, just like she did."

"Well, honey," Mom said, laughing, "we'll be right there, holding the stepladder, but I doubt you'd fall."

Stone nodded. "I think Mary Cassatt was thinking of Eve eating the forbidden fruit in the Garden of Eden. Once it had been eaten, she had as much right to the world as any of us."

CHAPTER THIRTEEN

When Loni's hospital time was up, Stone drove to Pittsburgh to take us home.

As we stepped out toward Stone's Chevy, there was a strange man standing at the curb door.

Loni elbowed me. Then she whispered, "It's Stone! He shaved off his whiskers."

Now, that was startling. He looked so different, I would walk right by him close up on the street, I honestly would. His face seemed to be longer and thinner, cheekbones sharp, because he wasn't as tanned where his beard had been shaved off. He looked yea younger, which just might sink him with Mom.

He was dressed up, too. No old khaki shirt. He had a blue sports jacket slung over the shoulder of a striped shirt. As he swung 'round to open the door, I expected his khaki pants to crack at the creases, they were pressed to such a faretheewell. His brown shoes were buffed to the nines.

Mom blinked when she saw him close shaved, and then we all bust out laughing. Even Stone huffed a laugh.

"I said, Why not?" Stone dragged at his face. "This beard comes and goes."

In the car, Stone asked, "Does it hurt much, Loni?"

She had a bulging patch over her eye socket and an

armful of drawing stuff the clinic gave her. I wished I could go to the hospital just once and get free stuff.

"It pulls and pinches," Loni said. "And it feels full. Dr. Mundell says that's the conformer."

"Tell Stone what a conformer is," Mom said.

"It's a piece of plastic over the implant to keep the socket open. Under this bandage, I really look like the Queen of Halloween. Blunked out, worse than Orphan Annie. They keep it in until I get my fake eye."

"Oh, don't say fake," Mom winced. "Say prosthetic, although I don't care diddly for that either."

"Prosthetic is pathetic," Loni rhymed, smiling.

"You said the conformer is over the implant," I said. "What's the implant anyway?"

"Okay," Loni said. "I made Dr. Mundell show it to me. It looks just like a button made of the screen from our screen door. But it's made of stuff that won't corrode."

"Tantalum mesh," Mom said. "I hope I pronounced it right."

"That's it," Loni said. "He says I won't feel it, but they even sew the eye muscles right into the mesh button, and the button moves when your muscles move right and left. My fake—prosthetic, okay, Mom?—eye will fit right over the button and move too. It sure sounds ucky, doesn't it. Little Orphan Annie. That's me."

CHAPTER FOURTEEN

"P̄etey," Loni asked spit-point after I took her supper up on a tray, "did you tell Stone that Mom didn't like his beard?"

"I did not. I'm not a squealer. Honest to God and hope to die, I did not. Did you?"

"Of course not!"

She dragged her fork over Mom's pepper and veal stew.

"Maybe he just wanted to look especially nice for her," she said.

"Or maybe Mom was staring funny at his beard," I said, "and it made him nervous."

"Oh, nice, Petey." Loni tapped the edges of her eye patch, all around, like she was tacking it down. "You sure have a romantic nature."

After supper, we thought Loni would rest, but she came downstairs, bringing her tray into the kitchen.

"Well, look at you!" Mom said. "Aren't you the one."

"I just thought I'd sit on the swing with Petey and Toby and watch the sunset," Loni said.

Sure she did. I knew she was still hepped up about Stone's shaving. I had to admit that for conversation, you couldn't beat Stone's having shaved. There's a whole evening's talk in someone who's shaved off a beard.

"Fresh air will do you good," Mom said, holding a

wet glass up from the soapy dishwater. She spun the glass in the window light so a bubble formed on its lip.

"Look at that little sun!" she exclaimed, staring into the sparkling bubble. "Your Dad used to say 'The best time of day is when that old sun goes down total. Then a peachy glow comes up and just a tint of lime green washes the sky. That's when the blue is best,' he'd say. 'Cobalt.'"

"But you didn't finish, Mom," I said. "He'd say, 'Cobalt. As blue as your mamma's eyes.'"

We all laughed, but Mom then quickly turned her back on us and bent her head. We shamed out of the kitchen to keep from seeing her cry.

Out on the porch, it was Dad's sky, all right. But bright as it was, it dampened us. When the lime edged into the blue, we stopped swinging. I was hoping the Ghost Car would *pah-pah* the driveway, but it never came. We waited. Nothing. When the bugs tuned up, we skipped off the swing and went inside.

Loni got out the Chinese checkers. We set the marbles in two of the starred points and began to play on the dining room table. Toby gave out a big sigh— *bor-ing!*—and padded off to the kitchen to sleep. With only two players, Chinese checkers is kind of boring. With six players, you have a whole bunch of marbles to jump through to get to the other side. With two, it takes a while to get enough marbles in the field to make hopping and stepping interesting.

But we weren't bored right off. There was a yea lot of conversation yet to cover with Stone's shaving his beard.

"I wonder if he uses a straight edge like Dad, or a safety razor," Loni said, twirling a marble in her fingers.

"I would think in the army," I said, making a step move, "you'd have to use something like Burma Shave in a tube. You wouldn't have room in your knapsack for Dad's shaving mug and soap."

"Let alone a moustache cup," Loni said, lifting her next marble and sniffing it precious, like it was a chocolate ready to be eaten. "Whatever that is."

"For fake moustaches, I think," I said.

I hopped over my first marble.

"Wouldn't it be hard to shave a whole beard without cutting the long hair off first?" Loni held her next marble over her bandage, pretending to peer through it like a glass eye. Hop.

"I never thought of that, but it would be, wouldn't it?" Step.

"How come pulling hair hurts, but cutting doesn't? Cutting should be worse." Hop.

"Yeah," I said, then changed the subject. "I bet Mom thinks Stone is awful young for her now that he is shaved."

"Stop saying that," Loni said. She picked up a marble and stepped it all across the board because there wasn't anything yet to hop.

"That's cheating!"

"Oh, Petey, this game is boring."

"Are you trying to get them married?" I said. "'Cause that's what it sounds like, you traitor!"

"Cripe's sakes, Petey, can't Mom have a good friend in her life without you getting green eyes?"

CHAPTER FIFTEEN

A week after Loni's operation, a cloudy July day, was a cloudier one for Mom. We were at the kitchen table. Toby was sitting up, begging for something from Loni's luncheon tray. Loni was drawing upstairs.

Mom had an open letter in her hand. A worrying look shot a dart between her eyebrows. I sensed there was trouble in that letter, but I had some worrying thoughts on my own mind.

"Mom," I said, sliding the tray toward me, "I heard the Ghost Car again last night."

"Oh, dear," Mom said, clapping the letter against her forehead. "The Ghost Car. Honey, please, I am in no mood for the Ghost Car."

Toby chuffed, and Mom blew up.

"Toby, you get under that stove this minute." He fell sideways off his haunches, *real* slow, flopping on his side, front paws still in begging position. *I'm dead.*

"You don't believe I can hear the Ghost Car, Mom?"

"Yes, but I don't believe you're hearing a ghost."

Mom set the letter on the table and drew her fingers around its edges, making a frame.

"Look, honey, cars from Cokin get lost up here in the daytime. So don't be surprised to hear them at night."

"Mom, I call it a Ghost Car because I never see it. I mean I hear it, but every time I lift the blind, it's gone.

That's why I call it a ghost."

"Petey. I don't believe in ghosts."

"We used to pray to the Holy Ghost at St. Jude's." In truth, without a car, we didn't go much to church anymore. But since Dad was Presbyterian, we were only half-Catholic anyway. Mom still made us say our prayers.

"That's different. Honey, please take the tray up to Loni. Oh, dear, I forgot the coffee! I can't get used to Loni wanting coffee. Well, our ration'll cover it."

"Maybe it's Dad, come down to guard us."

"Oh, Petey!" Mom slapped the letter down on the table. The faucet squealed as she filled the aluminum coffee pot. The Jewell coffee bag crackled as she measured the fresh grounds into the percolator.

"Well, geeszoy, if it's a comfort to you, it's a nice thought. I do believe you are still hard mourning Dad, as is proper, and maybe that's what this ghost car business is about. Why don't you just pray for Dad?"

"I do, Mom. But is it okay to pray *to* Dad?"

"Well, of course, you want to pray—to? Did you mean *to*?"

"I mean, I know we're supposed to pray *for* him, but is it okay to pray *to* him. To ask him for things. We pray to saints, and Dad was just as good. I mean, he didn't go to church, but that's not a mortal sin for Presbyterians. Dad drove us up to St. Jude's. He made us study the catechism and all. Dad was as good as anybody."

"Oh, honey, geeszoy, if there's a heaven, your father's

there or getting there. I don't see why you can't pray to him. Are you thinking of praying to him about Loni?"

"Yes. That. And to help me cross that dang trestle. It's hard to think of Dad looking down on us from heaven the whole livelong day and not doing anything. Just sitting up there on a cloud or something and watching us worrying about Loni, hoping her eye will turn out all right, watching me trying to walk that dang trestle, watching you sewing your head off and us missing him every minute, and not being able to do one thing about it. That couldn't be *heaven* for him. He must be a nervous wreck."

Mom raised the gas flame under the percolator. "It's easy to think that, honey. But Father Tierney once said souls are in a whole diddly-different time frame. To them, our whole lives down here pass in less time than it takes to crack an egg. They only see what we'll become—in heaven with them."

"Mom, then someone up there's got to be paying more heed. I mean, it's not less time to us down here. It's just for-ev-er the way I see it."

"Oh, honey. It's not that bad. You have your whole sweet life ahead of you. I know Loni's going to be all right. Look how well it's turning out."

Mom took a cup from the cupboard and set it on the cabinet next to the coffee pot, now throwing up its dark brew into the glass knob. I wished it tasted to me as good as it smelled.

"And you mustn't worry about me," she said. "I love

to sew. If I couldn't work with my hands, make nice things, I would die. I don't know how people live who can't make things. That's why I have high hopes for Loni. She can draw. She has real talent. That's God's gift. And I want her to develop it. She will. I am set on it."

Then while the coffee cooled, Mom took up the letter again. Put it down. Took it up. Then stared at me, her eyes dark.

"Petey," she said, almost whispering, "I want to ask you something. But promise me true you'll say nothing of this to your sister or Stone."

My sister. When Mom called Loni my sister, I knew it was real troubling.

"Is something wrong with Loni's eye?"

"No, no, it's healing right faster than they expected. No, it's something else. I'll be blunt-nosed about it. Have you seen Stone hugging Loni?"

"Has Stone ever..." It was hard for me to shift gears. "Hugging her? Well ye-es, but..."

"When was that?"

"When she finished her drawing."

"Tell me about it."

"Mom-om, why are you asking?"

"Honey, I don't think it's a hill of beans, but I need to know. Someone says—Oh, just tell me."

"As I said, Loni finished her drawing over Sunday the day before we started to work at Stone's place. Instead of at the rock?"

Mom nodded.

"When we got there, Stone was sitting on his deck rail, drinking from a mug of coffee. He took Loni's drawing and set it down on the deck, the way he does, so he could get a faraway look at it. He was real surprised Loni had finished it. 'A-one,' he said, and shook his head back and forth. Then he stood up and gave Loni a big hug."

Mom exhaled a lung of air. "For heaven's sakes and hell's fire," she said, slapping at the letter with the back of her hand.

"Mom, was that wrong?"

"No, not the least. But I have to ask you these things, honey. Did Stone ever hug Loni or touch her a lot...or, or kiss her, when you were around?"

"No, Mom, he never did that. Just that once."

"Of course," Mom said, giving the letter another good slap.

"I never believed this one minute."

"Mom who said that? Who is that letter from?"

"I don't know if... Let me think about this. But now, honey, not a whispering word to your sister or Stone. I might have to ask Loni about this sometime, but not now. Geeszoy, it would be stirful trouble if they heard any of this."

"Mom," I said, "I'm not a squealer. I bet it's that rat Olenk."

Mom looked down at me and shook her head.

"I don't know if I should tell you this, but it's Gen who wrote this."

"Gen Geeter!"

"The man himself. He says a number of things."

"Oh, sure. Sure! Gen Geeter was sitting on his porch, looking right over at us when Loni got hugged."

Mom's face went still. She sat down in a chair.

"He also said he saw them hugging on the rock."

"Mom, I was always with them on the rock."

Mom said, "We'll just see who's cooking cabbage up at Gen's."

The next minute she was on the phone to Gen Geeter.

"Gen, it's important I talk to you about your letter. No, I understand, not on this hook-up. I'll be up in the morning when Loni and Petey come up for their lessons with Stone."

Mom listened, frowning.

"I understand that," she said. "But I also think there are things you should know."

CHAPTER SIXTEEN

Mom hiked up One-Mile Path to Gen Geeter's with us, leaving Toby at home barking in protest. *I need to protect you!*

"Mom, why do you have to see Gen Geeter?" Loni asked.

"There are things we need to get fixed," she said to Loni, real nonchalant, "and it might be nice to see Stone's drawing. He said he's ready to pounce."

"Pounce?" I asked. I had slept poorly, or I should say I slept every which way but for real. I was worried for Stone and nervous for Mom having to talk to Gen Geeter about his mean letter.

"Stone's going to punch holes in the drawing," Loni said, "so he can trace it on the mural wall."

Stone was waiting for us on the porch, beaming that Mom had come up with us.

"I won't take the mural down until you're here, Alita," he said as she walked off.

I could see Gen Geeter pacing on his porch.

"I think I'll go outside and draw," I said to Stone and Loni. I was too addled to sit inside. I sat on a stone in line with Gen Geeter's porch and acted like I was drawing the corral. Now and then I looked over at Mom and Gen.

Mom held the letter in her hand as Gen talked. Then

Mom talked, her head bent to one side, like when she tries to get us to see her side of things. Finally, the worst thing happened. She got up and called out to me, motioning me to come up to the porch.

When I got there, Mom patted the pillow beside her on the glider. I sat down.

"Honey, Gen says you were not always with Stone and Loni on the rock. Is that the living truth?"

"I was so," I said. "Mom, you wouldn't let Loni come up there without us together."

"Now hold it, Son," Gen barked, doing his FDR imitation. "The last time you were on the rock with Stone and Loni, didn't you go off in the woods for a while?"

"Oh. I—I just went off to hunt for a balancing stick. Not for very long."

"There. You see," Gen said to Mom.

"No, I don't see, Gen. Your letter was out-and-out suggesting that Stone was—oh—being personal, as you put it, with Loni on many occasions."

Mom read from the letter. "'Hugging her and being personal with her on numerous occasions' is the way you put it. And then, Gen, you go on to say, 'I believe—'"

"All right," Gen said, interrupting and shifting in his chair. His face was as red as beet water.

Mom shook the letter at Gen.

"Let me finish. You go on to say, 'I believe Stone has an eye for Loni.' A smart choice of words, Gen, given

Loni's problem, and just, just pitiful, in my opinion."

"Did I say that? All right, I'm sorry. I never think of that girl as, ah, missi— that way. I do plead guilty for making assumptions from the occasions I witnessed."

"And what did you witness on that rock exactly when Petey went to get a stick?"

"Look, Ali, I enjoy walking my property. I was walking in the woods, back on that bluff above the rock. Stone had his arm around Loni and his head up against her face. And I know Petey saw them that way when he came out of the woods."

"Did you, Petey?" Mom asked.

"Yes, but they weren't hugging."

"Well, son, he wasn't just smelling her perfume."

"Gen, if you please," Mom said. "Petey, tell us what you saw when you came out of the woods to the rock."

"Loni was holding up the glass plate with the squares. Stone was leaning in, trying to see the trestle as Loni saw it."

I explained how Stone teaches drawing with the glass plate.

I put my arm over Mom's shoulders and put my head near hers. I held up my hand like I was looking through Loni's glass, sharing it with Mom.

I said, "Miss Calderwood in drawing and other teachers put their arm over your shoulders when they sit aside you trying to show you something. It doesn't mean they like you. It's the only way they can get close in. The other way, your shoulders would bump and you wouldn't fit on the seat."

Mom said, "From where you say you were standing in the woods, looking down, Gen, you might not have seen that glass plate, or what they were doing."

Gen's ears were feverish red. "No I didn't see any glass plate. But what of it? What was I supposed to think? And Ali, if I believed as I did, wasn't I obliged to tell you? Wrote the letter because I didn't want to use the party line."

"I don't know." Mom said. She turned to me. "Petey, you can go, and remember what I said. Not a diddly word to Loni and Stone."

I left, but only to the bottom of the steps and aside the stone wall that held up the porch. I was afraid for Mom to be by herself with mean Geeter.

I heard a chair scrape on the porch.

"I'm sorry, Gen," Mom said, "I happen to believe those things you think were so threatening to Loni were innocent, plum proper, and even kind. And I hope none of these suspicions of yours get back to Stone and Loni."

"Okay," Gen said. "If you want to put an innocent light on things. But I'll tell you one more thing. This sweetheart of yours—"

Mom broke in. "Sweetheart! He's a good friend, Gen, and he's caring of my kids. Something you could never bring yourself to be. Is that what this is all about?"

Gen lowered his voice.

"Stone's getting mental help at the vets hospital up in Pittsburgh. You should know that, Ali. If you want your kids exposed to that, go ahead. I wash my hands of it."

"Mental help!" Mom's voice was angry. "Like a lot of our boys, Gen, he's ricocheting from a breakdown. He was tortured nearly to death by Japanese soldiers, chained down in a Philippine prison camp. They put him in a corrugated tin box, pounded on it, broke every one of his ten fingers, Gen.

"Doctors believe it's a small stroke or something that makes him stutter. He was one of the few to ever escape and live to tell about it. I'm surprised as blazes at you, Gen, and I think I better be going."

CHAPTER SEVENTEEN

"Sorry I had to pull you into that, Petey," Mom said as we walked back to Stone's place.

"What did he mean about Stone's being mental?"

"Oh, were you listening? I don't like you ear holing, Petey."

"But, Mom, I was afraid for you. Gen Geeter's got guns."

"What's done is done. But not a word about the torture, any of this to Stone or to Loni. Stone could hardly put two words together about all he went through in those prison camps. But he wanted me to know."

It's okay for Stone to be your swee— *friend*, Mom. I don't think Dad would mind."

"Oh, honey, we are"—she shrugged and made a comic face—"friends. That's all."

This time, I noticed, she didn't say anything about her "puny scarecrow" education.

At Stone's, the air smelled of turpentine. Loni was leaning over her painting on the counter. A glass plate with dabs of colors and an old wooden box of oil colors in crinkled metal tubes was sitting beside her. The tubes looked like they were two hundred years old, oozing oil and all. Stone had picked them up at an auction, like a lot of his art supplies.

"Alita," Stone said pointing up to his drawing for the

mural, "there's my raggedy-A cartoon."

"Raggedy A, that's a hot one," I said, and we all had to laugh because it was raggedy, with pieces glued on, some with torn edges.

"I never heard *that* expression before," Mom said.

"I call B-Boony that. We called the line Marines that, only it's not as nice. We spelled out the A." Stone slapped his rear end.

"Raggedy-ass?" I guessed, then covered my mouth.

They all laughed.

But that drawing just knocked me for a loop, with all the black charcoal lines showing the whole valley, the steel mills streaming smoke, the trains, the bridges and trestle, the river with barges, vats pouring steaming steel, and up close, steelworkers with big muscles taming the hot metal. Perfect.

"Geeszoy!" Mom said. "Why Stone, it's changed so, and powerful. I like the way you've tied things up together, that roll of steel becoming the river. I'm speechless."

"Thank you, Alita. I've learned a lot by looking at the Mexican muralists," Stone said, reaching over to the bottom corner of the drawing with a screwdriver and prying out tacks.

"Now," Stone said, holding the corner of the drawing away from the wall, "if I had a pounce wheel, I'd roll it along these lines to make my tracing holes. But since I don't, I'll do it manually by jabbing holes through the paper."

He dropped the drawing and reached 'round to the corner of his work table and held up a tool that looked like an ice pick with a round handle.

"Like this," and he began punching holes in the drawing.

"Oh, you'll tear it to smithereens!" Mom said.

"It gets worse," Stone said. "When I tack it to the wall down at Cokin Steel's admin building, I'll have to dust it with ink powder called pounce. Then when I lift it off, I have a general idea where I want to go. But it is one black drawing."

"Only a general idea?" Mom asked.

"He'll have to do it all over again, Mom," Loni said. "That's what would get me. Right on the plaster."

"What if you make a mistake?" I said.

"I'll cover it over," Stone said, prying out more tacks.

"Remember, this is secco: the paint is applied to the dry plaster wall. Now, what is hard is *buon fresco*, where you work in wet plaster."

"I bet you could do that too," I said.

"You think so, Pete?" Stone smiled. "How about helping me untack this. I think I have all the rip cords taken care of. There are some screwdrivers in that drawer."

"Rip cords?" Loni asked.

"That's what the flyboys call loose ends."

We all got prying tools and helped Stone untack the raggedy-A cartoon. Then we held it while Stone climbed onto a stool and untacked the top. It folded over like a tattered and mended old bed sheet, poofing charcoal dust as it slid to the floor. Stone folded it in half, then in fourths, then over twice again, pressing it down like it was a raggedy-A piece of rusted scrap.

"Now," he said, "I'm ready for the wall."

CHAPTER EIGHTEEN

"Wake up, wake up, Petey," Loni whispered, "I hear a car. They're home. Let's get upstairs. Quick!"

We had moseyed into the living room and fallen asleep.

I staggered and stumbled up the stairs with Loni pushing me from behind. We turned off the light in my room and looked down. But there were no headlights.

"Shhh, Loni. The Ghost Car!"

And there it was, in the moonlight, a pale greenish top-down convertible flickering through the trees of our driveway. We couldn't tell who—what—was driving it.

Loni's hand pressed across my chest. Then it slid up to my mouth.

"Don't let it see your teeth," she mumbled close to my ear. She was talking through her free hand. "You die if ghosts see your teeth."

"Not if it's Dad," I said, my hand over my mouth.

"Petey," Loni said through her fingers. "It's hard to tell."

Pah-pah-pah. The Ghost Car all but disappeared behind the rose of Sharon thicket that edged our front yard. A flashlight blinked on and then off, and then it died as the sound faded into the woods.

"Loni," I whispered through my hand. "What exact color was it?"

"Greenish. It's the moonlight making it look greenish.

Hey, it could be yellow. It could be Gen Geeter."

"Darn," I said. "I wanted the Ghost Car to really be a ghost, maybe Dad, not ol' No Trespass."

I groused to bed and drifted off. Toby's barking woke me up. That would be Stone and Mom.

Mom came up soon after to check on us.

"I'm going to make Stone a cup of coffee," I heard her say to Loni.

I pretended to be asleep when she cracked the door to my room. I waited until she leaned over me. Then I whispered in a spooky voice, "I knooooow who the Ghost Car belongs to."

"You do? You do?"

"It's No Trespass Geeter."

Mom was smiling and her face was flushed. I guess Loni had told her.

"Well, we didn't actually see No Trespass. But it was a convertible, and it could have been yellow."

She sat on the side of my bed and looked off at my window.

"Could be," she said. "Maybe he's afraid we'll burn his house down. He is an air raid warden, you know."

"But there wasn't any drill or siren tonight," I said. "And not the other nights, either. I don't like people who pretend to be ghosts."

"Nobody likes to be spied on," Mom said. "But it's better than having strangers driving through here. Now try to sleep. I want to get Stone some coffee."

Stone came down to our house every evening now that his work was at the mill. Gen Geeter said he didn't want us in Stone's studio without supervision. Didn't want to be sued or anything if we set the place on fire.

Loni had to move her painting things to our basement and work under a dangling bulb.

"No matter," Stone said. "I can give you pointers in the evening, Loni. Can't change Geeter. He's set in his ways."

"Stone," Mom said, "Gen Geeter's more than set in his ways. He's pretty nibby. If I were you I'd be careful what I say on the phone."

Mom was smart to warn Stone. He'd be jumping mad if he really knew what Gen Geeter said about his hugging Loni.

"Hmmm, Alita," Stone said, "you really think he listens? Maybe we should blow some hot smoke on that phone, give him an earful."

Mom laughed. "Don't you daren't dare."

"You know something," Loni said, "I'd rather paint in that musty old cellar than go up to Gen Geeter's with you not there, Stone."

"Thank you, Loni," Stone said, beaming.

Mom was exchanging meals for Stone's little lessons at night. Having Stone around, sitting in Dad's chair and all, was something I had to get used to. But I decided I had to think of Mom and try not to show it. I got to thinking, too, of what Loni went through. How much better it was that she gave in and went through with another operation. If she could change, I didn't know why I couldn't.

I did like Stone. He'd come down to the house washed up, smelling of Lava soap. Packing his pipe with tobacco, fingernails still carrying some paint dibs and dabs, he'd light it up and coax it while we listened to the news with Lowell Thomas. We even got him to yell out ol' Lowell's deep booming sign-off, "So long until tomorrow."

The news was full of war stuff. We were winning on all fronts, as ol' Lowell liked to say. But Stone and Mom mostly talked politics at supper. Dewey was already nominated by the Republicans, but neither one, Mom or Stone, believed he could beat Roosevelt. The President was going to be a shoo-in for the Democratic convention coming up Monday and that was fine with them.

The really good news was that Loni's implant healing time was up. Mom wouldn't let Stone drive us to Pittsburgh, only as far as the Cokinville Greyhound bus station.

"Listen, Stone, we've taken up enough of your time. You've got to get on with that mural. Denny Dorfapple has offered to drive us home, and Brown's is letting him use their van."

"Now what did you do, Loni?" I asked as Denny Dorfapple drove us home from Pittsburgh. Denny was so tall he barely could get his head inside the van, and he blushed and gulped his Adam's apple every time Mom talked to him. As I said, he would be a perfect stork for Walt Disney.

Loni said, "He took out the conformer and made a mold of the inside of my eye. An eye fingerprint, he called it."

"Did it hurt?"

"Not really. Used a kind of jelly stuff."

"Now what?"

"He's going to make a plastic shell from the eye print. And then—ta-da!—he's going to show me how he paints the iris. Dr. Soliti knows I want to be an artist, so I get to watch."

Then Loni tapped Mom on the shoulder.

"Don't you think Stone would like to watch too?"

"I hate to ask him," Mom said. "I don't want him to feel obliged to drive us up here when he's got that mural to finish. I know how frazzled to the left gear I get when I'm trying to finish a drapery job. Don't I, Denny?"

"Uh-huh," Denny said, and even the back of his neck turned red. And that's about all I remember him saying that whole trip. I often wondered what he and Mom talked about when they carried her alterations to Brown's.

CHAPTER NINETEEN

When Mom told Stone about Dr. Soliti painting Loni's new eye the coming week, he insisted on driving us up.

"Oh, please," Loni begged. "Then we can see the mural."

"Stone," Mom said, "you're just too generous."

"I'm not being generous, Alita. I should make another hospital appointment, and I need to find more pigments for my mural."

We left early so we could have enough time to stop at Cokin Steel. Loni and me'd seen Stone's mural when it was only a dibbly-dot outline from the pouncing. Then a week later, just splats here and there of different colors.

"I st-started at the top and worked down," Stone said then. "I wanted to see how to balance my colors out."

It was yea different than his raggedy-A drawing, but Stone said it only seemed different. He had blown some things up and kind of let the air out of others.

"I was lucky," Stone said as we pulled into the parking lot behind Cokin Steel's dirty-buff brick administration building. "Bob Feller let me have a free hand all the way 'round. He's an early riser, so he just might be here."

The administration building had a blue-and-red army-navy E for Excellence flying beneath the flag out front.

At the entrance door, Stone held up his pass. A guard

who looked like a bulldog gave him a big gap-toothed smile.

"Family coming to see the mural, Stone?" he asked.

Stone nodded. He didn't say we weren't his family, which was nice. To be a family, even a fake one, was nice.

"Bob Feller's here," the guard said, pointing 'round to a tall white-haired man in a white shirt with flopping rolled-up sleeves and loosened tie. Now, right there, he'd be a perfect Clydesdale horse with white, fluffy hooves. He was flipping through some manila envelopes on a low table beside the guard's desk.

"Stone," he said, turning 'round, handing the guard an envelope, and holding on to some mail. "Assumed you were going up to Pittsburgh."

"I am. Stopped to give some friends a progress report."

Bob Feller remembered Mom and said our names.

"Coke plant's not the same without your husband running it, Mrs. Burns," he said.

Then he turned to Loni and me. "Look at the growth of you two." He shifted the mail to his left hand, offering his right hand to us like we were genuine grown-ups.

"Stone," he said, waving the mail at the mural. "You're making me look bad. It took me twenty years to build this mill, and you're building the whole valley in a month."

Stone huffed a laugh. "It's got a way to go," he said, moving the rope guard holders so we could get in closer.

The mural faced out on a kind of sitting place, couches and chairs down in a well. It was nice that people could sit down and look up at it. Right then, it made me think of a skeleton putting on his clothes. With the band of color across the top—blue sky, clouds with gold edges, and pinkish smoke—you could really see where Stone was heading. It was startling to see how bright it was going to be.

"Uh-oh," Stone said, sniffing the air.

There were coffee cans and a water jug lined up under the mural. Stone peered into one of them, then sniffed it.

"Sorry, Bob," he said, taking it and setting it aside. "Afraid we have a little rotten egg mixture here. I'll flush this away before I leave."

Loni and me held our noses.

"Now, it isn't that bad, you two!" Mom said.

Bob Feller had a booming laugh.

"Are you having any trouble getting eggs?" Bob Feller asked. Stone was using the yolks of eggs to mix with his colors. Didn't turn the colors yellow or anything; mixed just like water.

"Gosh, no," Stone said. "Plenty of cold-storage eggs, if I needed them. But I don't. Farmers around here don't know what do do with their eggs."

"Government has powdered eggs enough to fight two wars," Bob Feller said.

"Pigments are a different matter," Stone said. "Lucky

Strike green, as the ads say, has definitely gone to war. That means blue and yellow aren't easy to get, either. But I'll try to pick more up in Pittsburgh this trip."

"Let me know," Bob Feller said, waving and tearing into an envelope as he walked away down a hall. Then he stopped suddenly, whirled around, and yelled, "Hey, it says here the country has produced nearly 80 million ingot tons of steel since Pearl Harbor! Imagine that!"

CHAPTER TWENTY

"Okay, then," Commander Soliti said, peeling off his rubber gloves. They squealed and popped like roasting weenies.

"That plastic shell was a good fit, Loni," he said. "Now, I know what you've been waiting for. Let's all move over here to the drawing board, and we'll see about painting the iris disk."

"Loni, you sit right there, facing me on that stool."

Commander Soliti sat on a revolving chair at the drawing board. One sideboard had tubes of paint, a glass of brushes, a cutting knife and a little tub of water. The other side had a piece of glass.

Tacked to the board was a sheet of white paper with little white circles stuck down on it.

"These are your iris disks," Commander Soliti said. "I paint right on them, and then peel them off that sheet."

He tapped a little bull's-eye circle drawn in the center of each disk. Like a target.

"I don't paint the cornea; that's outlined by the circle in the center. I'll attend to that later."

"Are the disks watercolor paper?" Stone asked.

"Yes, the thinnest and smoothest. I tack them down with rubber cement. I add a thin coat of Chinese white on each disk."

He began sqeezing out little dabs of paint onto a piece of glass.

"Tube watercolors," Stone said, sounding disappointed. "You don't use dry pigments? I was hoping I could buy some from you."

"No, but I know where you can get them. It would be too much trouble to grind them into gum arabic. We have a good-quality supply of cake or tube colors. It could happen if shortages continue. But this is high-priority work."

"I do experiment with mixing Chinese or zinc white into the watercolors. We're really talking about gouache."

"Watercolor is my favorite," Loni said. "I'm glad you're not using ucky poster paint."

Stone and Commander Soliti laughed.

Commander Soliti pressed some more colors from the tubes.

"Those are a lot of colors," Loni said.

"Yes," he said, "that's for your hazel eye."

He pointed a brush at each dab of color, ticking them off. "Burnt umber, yellow ochre, oxide of chromium, crimson red, ivory black. And that's only for the background mixture."

"Wow, that many," Loni said.

"Oh, there's more," Commander Soliti said. "I use different combinations for the collarette, the little ring around the pupil. I'll add titanium white and cobalt blue to the yellow and red. Then there's the stroma. Everybody knows what the stroma is."

"Oh, sure," Loni said, kidding. And we all laughed.

"The stroma is the big color area of the eye. When they say you have a hazel eye, Loni, they mean the stroma. You have a blue edge around your iris, and I'll do that now."

Commander Soliti was fast. He laid on a circle of blue, not caring that he slopped paint outside the disk. "That edge will be clean as a whistle when I peel this disk off the background paper," he said.

Then he mixed his paints to the right shade for the darkest part of Loni's eye color, the color of a green olive. He painted over most of the blue, leaving a thin blue line inside the sloppy edge.

Next, he filled in the circle halfway to where the center cornea would be, leaving a teeny wedge of white.

"Okay, Loni," he said. "See this white speck? You get to paint that."

"Oh, I—" Loni pulled back a strand of hair. "Oh, I think I could do that."

"Just a dab," Commander Soliti said, handing Loni his brush.

She stood up, took the brush from him, and making little eeky sounds in her throat, dabbed out the little wedge of white.

"Whew," she said, blowing out some air.

"Perfect," Commander Soliti said. "Now you can say

you helped paint your eye."

Then he untacked it and put it on a heated tray for a few seconds. When it was dry, he painted in another greenish ring around the edge, the collarette, and dried that.

"That white center bull's-eye makes it look like a dead fish's eye," Loni said, sounding sad.

"Right," Commander Soliti said, "but in a minute, it won't. Pretty soon, I'll punch that center cornea right out.

"Now," he said, "we'll try to bring this to life."

He peered real deep into Loni's eye. Then, with a tiny, pointy brush, he began to make yellowish sparkling lines out from the white center. Some of the lines slopped right into the white bull's-eye.

He blew over the sparkling lines to help them dry faster. He then picked up a paper punch and snapped out the white bull's-eye center, leaving a clean hole.

He slid the hole over a shiny black sheet of paper.

"Now that's your cornea," he said, pressing his thumbs on each side of the eye to hold the paper down.

"Ahhh," Loni said.

"Oh, it's not done," Commander Soliti said. "When it's done, it will shine, like a real eye. This little donut iris gets laminated on the shell right over the black cornea center."

"That's amazing," Stone said, looking at the painting of Loni's eye.

Commander Soliti held the painted sheet over Loni's

eye socket. He rocked his head, trying to see if he got a good match with the other eye. He set the drawing back down on his drawing board and drew pencil lines out from parts of the painted iris, scribbling notes.

"I'll work some more on this before I peel it off. I think you'll be pleased, Loni."

"I'm already pleased," Loni said, nodding.

"Now when I paint the sclera—the white—we even put in the tiny veins," he said. "Fine rayon threads. I won't do that now, and I won't use many veins for someone as young as you. But I have to lay down the law with some of these hard-drinking vets. I say, 'No hangovers the day I have to match your eye. I don't intend to use a whole roll of thread to match the bloodshot.'"

Commander Soliti chuckled over his little story.

I meant to check the looking glass when I got home to see if I had any veins, because I sure didn't remember any.

As we were about to leave, Commander Soliti said, "Your eye should be ready in a week Monday. Laminating, finishing and polishing. I believe you're going to have a fine eye, Loni."

Loni nodded. Her face was still, and she said very little on our way home. I wondered if she'd like it, wear it once she had it.

CHAPTER TWENTY-ONE

Stone's mural was halfway done when Loni got her new eye.

Commander Soliti sat her in the revolving enamel chair with her back to us. She was close up to the commander and he was against the cabinets. Me, Mom, and Stone could only stand to the side. Couldn't see much of her eye at all.

Commander Soliti fitted and fiddled the shell over her implant.

Then he peeled off his rubber gloves. He raised his hands and stared into Loni's face like Mr. Westerhouse of the Logan Glee Club. Staring, staring, daring, daring anyone to even blink. Slowly, slowly, he reached 'round behind him to a looking glass propped up on his cabinet.

His blind fingers tickling the air, he nearly knocked the looking glass off its wire stand. We all reached out, Mom's hands shaking like Jell-O. But Commander Soliti caught it, set it right, and brought it up to Loni's face.

We leaned 'round and craned in to see Loni.

"I won't say a word," he said.

He needn't have. It was perfect. It looked like Loni had waked up for the first time, two startling hazel eyes seeing the world clean and new as a baby.

Loni's hand went up to her mouth and her head went down. She shook, crying.

"Oh, now," Commander Soliti said, pretending to be mad, "are you going to ruin this presentation? I can't do much for red eyes."

Mom came 'round and put her arm around Loni's shoulders. But she was crying, too, her mouth gaping for air.

What made me mad is, something welled right up in me without asking leave. Stone had to grip my shoulders hard to keep me from shaking apart.

Just then Raggedy-A Boone came in, balancing on his hook a cake lit with two candles. He had been hiding in the waiting room the whole time, waiting to spring in at the right moment.

"Whoaaaa," he said. "What is this? Someone die?"

"Born, more like," Stone said.

CHAPTER TWENTY-TWO

Loni's eye was a perfect match. The implant made it move together with the other as natural as the eyes in the cat clock in Wermer's Jewelry. Of course, I wouldn't say that to Loni, as it made it sound like her eye looked fake, and it didn't.

The neat thing to me was, she could sleep with it. Do just about anything. Although Commander Soliti cautioned her about swimming underwater. Loni was never an underwater swimmer anyhow, so that wasn't much of a caution.

I bet you can't imagine what she said to Stone a week or so after she got it.

"This eye is real nice, but not as distinctive as the patch, is it Stone?"

"Now, there's an artist," Stone said, laughing.

That afternoon I went out in the woods and cut me a straight sapling, trimmed and skinned it.

I didn't say a word to Mom, Stone, or Loni. It was something I had to do alone. Then, pretending to be only taking Toby for a walk, I picked up my sapling stick and headed for the trestle.

I hooked Toby's lead to a spike, checked his collar, which we always kept loose to keep him from strangling if he got caught on something. While he whined, I set out on the trestle.

I raced along the surface ties until I hit the section where the ground sloped off. Then I had to watch so I wouldn't trip.

Where the bank dropped sharp, my heart began to pound. Prickly needles traveled over my hands. They seemed to be sucking the blood right out of my palms.

My mouth went dry.

Balance, balance the pole. You can't fall, you can't fall with this pole.

Think of something you like, didn't Stone say? I thought of elevators, riding up in the clinic, the old black operator singing the floors.

First flo-or—I stepped. Second. Third.

Uh. Uh.

Now the white water, way, way down. I edged forward, trembling. My hands were wet against the damp-skinned wood. My feet were so light. L-Light. I could hardly put one—more—foot—down.

I stopped. Closed my eyes. Had to open my mouth to breathe. My heart hop-danced, danced, danced.

Lift legs, I told myself. Lift!

Won't lift.

A bead of sweat came down over my eye. Dripped off my lashes and fell down my cheek.

I licked at it. Mad.

"I-I am *not*," I shouted, "Crying. NOT."

Shouting revved me up again.

Then an awful needling voice sang out behind me.

"I am not crying." It was Olenk.

"Hup, two, three, four," he shouted. The voice closing in on my back.

I stepped out, trying not to look down. Down, down.

The cradle was just ahead.

I'd be safe in the cradle. But I already did that. Did that. He would not force me down into that.

His voice grew closer. He began to sing. "'From the Halls of Montezummmma to the shores of Tripoli.' Hup, hup, hup, sis, hup. 'We will fight our country's battlllles on the land and on the sea.'"

Then he stopped short and shouted, "Hey, cut it out, cut it out."

I heard Toby growling and yipping. Uh-oh. Gotta-sing-gotta-dance Toby had slipped his collar.

"Call your dog off," Olenk shouted, "or I'll kick him over."

"You—you better start dancing and get off," I shouted, standing stock still. "Or he'll bite."

Toby danced 'round me now. He'd stay with me.

I took a deep breath—Stone's idea.

Can't go back. Olenk back there. Couldn't turn around if I wanted to.

Just as far to go back.

Toby stood, panting, worrying at me and then swinging his head forward. *I smell your fear, but I am here.*

Stepped out again. One tie. Again. Two. Again.

Oh, God. I slid over something. Didn't need to look down to know my shoe had come untied. But looked down anyhow to keep from tripping. Under my laces— way down—rocks! I had crossed the creek!

Water rolled down my face.

Step, step, step. The heck with my shoelace.

Green now. Weeds. Then the gravel came up. Up.

Easy, easy, easy, easy. Hup, one, two. I slapped my gym shoes down so hard they stung my soles.

All level now. I danced to the end, grabbing Toby's collar. Spun 'round with my stick to face Olenk. But he was gone, gone.

Sitting on the other side, back on the rail of the overpass, a smile lighting his face like a jack-o'-lantern, was Stone.

CHAPTER TWENTY-THREE

Perfect. Just perfect.

But then, just as things looked almost perfect, sad word came to one of Mom's friends.

"None of us escape this world of tears," Mom said, getting off the phone. She was dabbing at her eyes.

"Sarah Link's boy, the one who was wounded on Tarawa. He died at the vets hospital in Pittsburgh."

Sarah Link was a presser at Brown's. A widow like Mom, she was one of Mom's friends there.

"At least she'll have him home," she said.

When the viewing began, Stone drove us up to Cokinville. Past the buff-colored brick building where his mural was. Then on to the old mill part of town, where Mrs. Link lived.

"Could be a storm," Mom said as Stone turned the Chevy's wheels into a hill curb to park.

I blew some of the soot off the Chevy sill before rolling the window up to a crack. The door handles outside were so hot I had to dance my fingers off the metal and slam the door by slapping the wooden panels.

"Does it get this hot in Washington state, Stone?" I asked.

"In Pasco, but not Seattle. Cool there. 'Summer school where summer's cool' is a slogan the university uses. But it's clean and the Sound air is wonderful. Rains a lot in winter."

"Is it pretty?" Mom said. "Should I aim my sights for Seattle?"

"I would," Stone said.

I wish he had said "Yes, come with me," but he didn't.

Mom, me, and Loni walked up to the Links' house.

Stone walked downhill to do some errands. He would reconnoiter with us at Isaly's. We didn't expect him to come with us to the viewing.

The air was filled with shiny bits of metal, like the stuff that floats in Christmas globes, only these were black and gritty. Mom worried aloud as we neared the Link porch about Loni catching grit in her new eye.

"Oh, Mom," Loni said smiling, "you know what Pollyanna would say. 'At least I can take my eye out and wash it. Something you and Petey can't do.'"

Then we all three started to laugh. When Loni was little, Mom gave her a copy of *Pollyanna*. She read it over and over. But as she got older, she started to make fun of it, especially Pollyanna's "glad game." When a friend broke his leg, Pollyanna thought he should of been glad because he didn't break both of them.

"Oh, we shouldn't be laughing," Mom said.

Just then, a car honked. It was an old, beat-up, white convertible with its tattered top down. Denny Dorfapple, Mom's errand boy, waved.

"Must be his day off," Mom said. "He's so shy, it's a wonder he honked."

He sailed by real slow, blushing all the way. *Pah-pah-pah.*

Mom pulled at my arm. "Here's the Link house."

The house was painted brown. To hide the dirt from Cokin Steel, I guessed. The roof porch sagged off downhill as the house tugged up. There were flowers hanging at the side of the open door, reminding me too much of Dad's funeral.

Inside, the whir of a turning fan and suffocating smell of lilies got to me right away. Sarah Link was all in black. She and Mom hugged and whispered a few words between the tears. She must've been at Dad's funeral, but I didn't remember her at all. She gave Loni a hug and stole a look at her eyes, so Mom probably told her at Brown's about Loni's operation. I wondered if she could tell which eye was which.

The bronze coffin was closed. There was an American flag over it. A gold star hung on a pole beside it. The whole room was banked with flowers with silver names on wide ribbons flowing across the baskets. Mom slid away from Sarah and led us to the kneeler to pray an Our Father and Hail Mary.

When we got up and turned around, there was Olenk staring at me. His mouth had fallen open, but no more so than mine, I guess.

"This is my youngest, Ossie," Mrs. Link said to us.

"I don't think you've met. Shake hands, Ossie. Mrs. Burns is number one in my book—yes, you are, Ali!"

Ossie. Ossie Link. O. Link. Olink. The rat Olenk. We never heard it right.

Me and Loni exchanged startled looks.

Then, Loni stepped right up to Olenk-Olink, leaned into his face and said, "Ossie, I'm very sorry about your brother."

I thanked God right there that she didn't say "Take a good look, punk. Remember me, I'm the Queen of Halloween" because it wouldn't have surprised me.

Olenk-Olink's face was a study. If I hadn't been there he might never've made the connection between the old Loni and the new Loni. But I could see his flushed, pudgy face was making it, all right. He mumbled something and backed away from us, turning and mumbling out of the room.

I walked out of that sad house torn up inside. At first I was glad something terrible happened to Olenk-Olink. Then I felt bad that I held such a thought, then sad that it'd happened to his mother.

I started to say something to Mom, but she had a handkerchief up to her mouth. Breathing hard. Sure, she was thinking of Dad's funeral.

Her crying choked us up, but Loni finally pulled me aside and strangled out, "Don't tell Mom about Olenk. It might cause hard feelings with his mother. And what good would it do now?"

"Olenk didn't recognize you at first, Loni,"

"I know, Petey. The Queen of Halloween has just struck out. Melted. Gone forever."

CHAPTER TWENTY-FOUR

Loni was down in the basement, painting and singing so loud I could hear her. Now that was a big change. Gotta-sing-gotta-dance Toby was at the cellar door, whining to be let down.

I was sitting in the dining room, half listening to Mom and Stone in the living room. They were having coffee after dinner.

My mind was on the Ghost Car. Ever since the Link funeral, something was nagging at me, and now I had it. I had it! The Ghost Car was Denny Dorfapple! *Pah-pah-pah*, passing us on the way to the funeral. He knew our driveway by heart. He was crazy about Mom. I jumped up and opened the cellar door. Toby scooted ahead of me. Then down the steps we scurried. I tripped on my laces halfway down. I was hurled in one flying shot to the bottom, almost landing on Toby.

"Loni, Loni," I said, picking myself up. "Loni, Loni, I know who drives the Ghost Car. It's Denny Dorfapple."

Then she gave me a frowning look.

"He doesn't drive a green convertible, does he?"

"No, the white convertible, outside Olenk's house. At the viewing. And I'd know that pah-pah sound anywhere."

"Of course. Gosh sakes! That white convertible could look greenish in the moonlight. What with all those bushes and trees around.

"Let's tell Mom and Stone."

We tromped upstairs, not caring about the noise we made, Toby flying between us. At the top, before opening the door, Loni shushed me, holding me back, and grabbing Toby's collar.

"Careful, they could be you-know-whating."

So I followed her, tiptoeing down the hall. We heard Mom and Stone laugh.

"Shhhhh," Loni said, as we both stopped just short of the French doors. We scratched Toby to keep him quiet. He slid over onto his back, his paws lolled up. He rolled his worrying eyes left and right. *Uh, uh, uh. Be serious, sweeties. Don't slight the good places.*

We could hear Mom talking about Gen Geeter.

"But, as I got my bearings," Mom said, "I saw how it could never be. I didn't care a fiddle for Gen. Money or no money. And what capped it was Gen's slant toward the kids. Downright fearful of Loni's medical expenses— well, he knew the mill picked them up—and her school problems. Nervous about the kids. Get hurt on his property and he'd be sued or something. Oh, who knows how that strange cat sings?"

It didn't seem like a good time to break into Mom's conversation. It was about us. We made faces at each other—should we stay or go?—but not wanting to arouse Toby if Loni stopped scratching him.

Mom went on, "But he *per*sisted. Crept around like a

fox on ice. He wanted me, but not the kids. Still does. He's sad. He'd give me this house, and I should live down here with the kids and be his—you know what— up there. And he couldn't see for blind bats why that wouldn't appeal to me."

"He's still jealous about you, Alita. Once he saw the kids coming up to the studio, his attitude toward me swung right about-face. Shoot, he started avoiding me. We recently tangled."

"What did he say?"

"Barked out, 'Why are you getting involved with Ali and those kids?'"

Mom laughed. "What did you say to that, Stone?"

Stone's voice got real serious and slow. "I said I was never happier than with you and the kids. I could live the rest of my life with you and the kids."

Loni's eyes got as wide as she dared make them, and she gave me a big, wild grin.

"Stone," Mom said.

"I mean it, Alita."

"But you have your schooling, and now with the G.I. Bill, it would be plum foolish to turn your back on it."

"I know. But I also know I hate the setup, living alone in barracks again. That's what they're planning for vets on campuses. Depresses me. Still feeling the box, I guess."

"You're a fine carpenter, Stone. Have you thought of doing that and painting on the side?"

"I didn't do one bit on that mural while I was remaking that damn carriage house of Gen's. One craft takes from the other. But with teaching, I think I'd be involved in painting all the time. The fine arts teachers at the university were like that."

"So you think of getting a fine arts degree? Not the architecture business?"

"Seems the best choice, but I think I'd crack up in a dormitory. It's this nightmare from prison camp, I guess."

"Stone," Mom said, "what if you lived in a house?"

"Pretty expensive."

"You could share."

Stone said, "Share? Maybe with a widow and her two children. Would you consider that, Alita?"

"Stone!"

"No, I'm proposing. *Marriage*, Alita. I want to marry you."

There was a long, ticking quiet. I wanted to break in right there, 'cause it was getting embarrassing, but Loni held my arm.

Mom said, "It's been a while since Pete died, but I still miss him. I want you to know that."

"I-I know, and why wouldn't you miss him? He was a good man."

"But I do love you, Stone. And it wouldn't be unfair to the kids, I know that now. They like you and respect you. But, oh, Stone, how would we live?"

"On love," Stone said, and they both laughed. "My disability check, my carpentry work while I'm in school, for one thing."

"Not up in Cokinville," Mom said. "And going back and forth to Pittsburgh you'd be dead as nails."

"Oh, no, not here, Alita. West. I've written to the University of Washington and they have just the program for me. And a lot of my old course work will count toward a Master of Fine Arts degree."

"Oh, Stone, West! Seattle! Geeszoy, I would think in a big city like that I could help you. There's Pete's pension, and I could get a lot of work in altering or maybe even in dressmaking. Oh..."

There was a pause.

I pushed Loni in.

Stone and Mom were hugging. You-know-whating, Loni would say.

Toby jumped up between them, and they jerked apart.

We stood there breathing hard, our eyes wet, and not knowing a single thing to say.

CHAPTER TWENTY-FIVE

Stone finished the painting for Cokin Steel. He had a big write-up in the Cokinville *Times*, with a picture of him hunkering in front of his mural. Bob Feller was so pleased he paid Stone twice what they'd agreed on. Then he gave Stone the keys to the Chevy and told him to keep the X stamp until it ran out.

It was the first time Stone was able to sit down with a reporter, telling the whole story of his capture and escape from Japanese soldiers in the Philippines.

The torture he had told Mom about was all there to make one sick to the stomach. They broke his fingers for trying to escape. The second time, he got away. Filipinos helped him get a *banca*, an outrigger canoe. He was lucky to be picked up by Navy frogmen from an American submarine and taken to Australia.

"I hope telling all that wasn't too hard on you, Stone," Mom said afterward.

"I wavered a little, talking to that reporter, but I got through it. I think the trembles and the nightmares and the sweats are nearly over, Alita. And going slow is helping me get over this stutter."

We know Gen Geeter read all about it. He asked Stone if he wanted the clipping from the *Times*. Then he thanked Stone for fixing up the carriage house. He sent Mom an apologizing note, but didn't say what about.

Said he wished her luck.

Mom and Stone's wedding was in Follansbee, West Virginia. It was real nice for a justice-of-the-peace wedding. Raggedy-A Boony was best man, and busted us all up by coming dressed to the nines in his red, white, and blue Marine uniform. Loni was maid of honor. They all four made a pretty picture. Now, Loni said I wasn't very romantic, but I got to thinking. Wouldn't it beat all if Loni and Boony got married someday—to each other.

I've been thinking about Olenk, too. He lost a brother in the war and never much knew his father, which wasn't an excuse but could be a cause for his being so mean. Maybe a wizard—maybe remembering Loni—will give him a softer heart. I hope so.

No need for Denny Dorfapple to have a softer heart. Mom never said a word to him about the Ghost Car. "He's shy and lonely," she said, "and he's been so nice to us all these years. So there was no harm in his driving by when the spirit moved him. I do believe he was looking out for us."

As for me, I won't ever have to walk that trestle again. I *am* glad I whipped it once, though. Wish I wasn't afraid of heights like that. But as Stone says, we're all born with something we'd like to change. All we can do is keep trying.

I can't wait to see Seattle. Loni and me and Mom will sing a lot on the trip West. I hope Toby doesn't expect us to dance in the Chevy.